River of Madness

by

William Hallstead

International Standard Book Number 13: 978-1-60452-086-6
International Standard Book Number 10: 1-60452-086-8
Library of Congress Control Number: 2014930251

BluewaterPress LLC
52 Tuscan Way Ste 202-309
Saint Augustine Florida 32092

http://bluewaterpress.com

This book may be purchased online at -
http://www.bluewaterpress.com/river

Printed in the United States of America

Also by the author
Raging Skies
Hard Days in Paradise

Writing as "William Beechcroft"

Position of Ultimate Trust
Image of Evil
The Rebuilt Man
Chain of Vengeance
Secret Kils
Pursuit of Fear

He took another step toward me. And grinned. "I should have got St. John to say a prayer for you." Then he burst into laughter. "Jesus, Durkin, you're about to die and you're standing here in rubber gloves holding—what in hell are those?"

"Poison-dart frogs. That's why the gloves, Ted." And his disgusted grimace gave me a flicker of hope. "Remember? I told you their sweat can kill. And these little bastards are damned nervous."

River of Madness

1

On the riverbank in Brazil's late December mugginess, I faced downstream, arms folded. And waited. In the past year and a half, I'd stood a hundred times on this 20-foot-high embankment overlooking the Trombetas. In its broad flow, in the sweet scent of tropical flora underlaid with the pungency of jungle decay, in the rain forest's chirps and buzzes, I found serenity.

But not today.

An idyllic two-year working sojourn. Unhurried scientific study. Hours of leisurely time together in a setting Hollywood would envy. Such was my and Felicia's expectation. But now, I—Emmett Durkin, chief of the Philadelphia-based Rebner Foundation's Research Station Four—felt something I had not experienced in all my months here. A chill. Worse. A sense of foreboding.

An odd reaction. Irrational, I tried to tell myself. The boat I'm waiting for is bringing the untrained screw-up nephew of the Foundation's chairman, Oliver Rebner. Nephew Theodore is being exiled here to "find himself." If a man hadn't found himself by the age of thirty, I thought, there couldn't be much to find. And if Theodore Rebner hadn't found himself a life in the City of Brotherly Love, how in hell was he going to find one here? On this backwater tributary hundreds of miles up the Amazon.

Why my queasiness this serene afternoon? Rebner's age? That he was four years my senior? It was more than that. I was a lab man. A researcher. Not cut out to be a station chief, I discovered early on, when I found myself using the Station's lab for escape from management trivia as much as for research. Fortunately, I was confident no one here would ever challenge me. Not our two Bororo Indian laborers. Not our mixed-breed housekeeper-cook. Surely not Felicia. But this guy—the chairman's failed nephew — was a damned unwelcome surprise, made more unsettling by the delay in Oliver's letter, dated three weeks ago but delivered here only the day before yesterday.

I hated surprises.

This ne'er-do-well was being exiled here. The fallout of a not altogether mutual involvement of himself and the no-longer-virgin daughter of one of Oliver's old frat brothers. That bit of info had come in a mailed scandalgram from the most ferret-like member of Felicia's upper crust friends. Uncle Oliver had delegated a family problem by making nephew Theodore my problem. Excluding his carnal activities, the man had no biology background whatever. "Ted is a Cornell graduate," the chairman wrote. "His major was hotel management."

Hotel management. Maybe in the rag-tag frame structures of our rainforest Astoria, Ted Rebner could see that our housekeeper-cook turned down our cot sheets at dusk and left a fresh orchid on our pillows. "Take him under your wing," Oliver's letter had directed. "Teach him what you can." Not "everything you know," But "what you can." A tip-off. This family embarrassment would be of limited mental prowess.

Think positive, Durkin. Maybe he would be just another scrawny little shit, no taller than I. Broken by his own inertia. Ready to be told what to do — if he can do anything at all. I squinted downriver, beyond our floating dock with its inverted green canoe and the Boston Whaler moored along the downstream side. Why was I wasting all this anxiety on a man who might, after all, fit in? Perhaps be an asset.

The toots of the steam launch whistle flushed a shrieking flock of macaws from the forest canopy. Darts of red, blue and yellow trailed across the river as the low-slung boat nosed around the south bend, spouting smoke from its outdated stack. At the wheel amidships, Capitán — a self-exiled Mexican, he insisted on Spanish in this Portuguese-speaking country — Gaspar Picos waved. I waved back, but my eyes were on the man standing at the bow. A big man. Surely over six feet and topping 200 pounds. At a wiry five-foot-seven, I already felt diminished.

The engine's chuffing slowed, died. The launch nosed shoreward, drifted to the dock. "No visita este tempo, Señor Durkin!" stubby, nut-brown Picos shouted. "I must go quick back to Oriximiná."

To the Indian deckhand who was shoving Rebner's luggage out on the dock, Picos yelled, "Rápido rápido, goddam!"

Picos had told me he hated these upriver runs, but he was ever-faithful to his schedule. Hated the Portuguese language, too, and stuck obstinately to "Spanglish." Just yesterday, Picos had radioed me about this unscheduled stop to drop off passenger Rebner. I assumed our pleasantries of his periodic cargo stops were not expected today.

Theodore Rebner stepped onto the floating dock, pointed at his three leather suitcases and a garment bag — a garment bag, for God's sake. He made lifting motions to the deckhand. Then he looked up at me, stepped toward the bank and tripped over his damned garment bag. A klutz? His crabwise climb up the weedy bank was an awkward performance, followed adroitly by the deckhand laden with his luggage.

Appearing as if he were rudely transported to this rustic outback straight from L. L. Bean, Rebner arrived panting at the bank's crest. His multi-pocketed safari chinos were travel-soiled. His broad-brimmed Anzac hat, rakishly pinned up on one side, was sweat-stained. He was a good-looking guy; I'd give him that. The late night movies' Errol Flynn without the mustache, in out-of-place safari costume.

"Theodore Rebner, I presume."

He ignored my hand. "Where do I find a biologist named Durkin? I'm supposed to—" A disbelieving frown swept across his chisel-chinned face. "You couldn't be him?"

I knew I looked unimpressive in my grubby jeans and Mote Marine T-shirt; hell, I was unimpressive even in more splendid dress. One of my college classmates called me "Woody Allen without glasses."

"Durkin in person," I assured him.

"Why in hell don't you build some steps up from the river?"

"Because the rainy season floods the river nearly up to this level." I struggled to keep my voice steady. "The dock floats up with it. The vegetation stabilizes the bank, but steps would be washed away. Welcome to Station Four."

Recovering from his huff-puff up the riverbank, Rebner thumbed back his Aussie hat and mopped his face with a red bandanna. Had that come as part of his "intrepid explorer" ensemble? The deckhand plunked down the bags and gave Rebner a burlesque salute, a lopsided grin, then muttered something uncomplimentary.

"What did he say? I don't speak Spanish."

"Neither does he. That was the Portuguese equivalent of 'have a nice day.'"

Well, not quite.

The crewman scrambled back down the bank, cast off the mooring lines and hopped aboard. With a departing toot, the grubby little boat puttered free of the dock, nosed into the river's current and swung downstream. I gave Picos a farewell wave and turned back to Rebner.

He still gasped for breath. His healthy northern winter glow, I suspected, was no doubt acquired in a Philadelphia tanning salon, then crisped around the edges by his recent lounging on the cruise ship's sparkling deck during its ramble up the Amazon to Oriximiná. There Rebner transferred to Picos's ratty wood-burner. At that turn of events, a degree of reality should have set in.

Despite the hat's wide brim, Rebner dramatically shaded his eyes. "Now that I'm here, exactly where in hell am I?" His deep voice sounded strained. I noticed he had a habit of jutting out his chin when he spoke. An actor's pose: a superior deigning to converse with a lesser being.

"Twenty-five miles up the Trombetas tributary from Oriximiná, the nearest town on the Amazon. And Oriximiná is four hundred air miles from the coast," I took some pleasure in telling him. "So you're pretty far up the creek, you might say."

"Christ. What is there to do around here besides whatever you do for the Foundation?"

Enjoying Rebner's dismay, I smiled benignly. "There's an opera house in Manaus, the closest city of any real size." I nodded at the beige garment bag. "Might have use for that up there."

"Where's Manaus?"

"Five hundred miles further up the Amazon."

"Jesus."

"Our local entertainment," I couldn't resist adding, "is watching the excursion boat from Oriximiná go north to Lake do Erepecu on Tuesdays, come back down on Thursdays. Too far across the river to hear, though. And when it's hazy, you can't even see it."

"Excursion boat? So why couldn't I have come up on that instead of that clown's scruffy little barge?"

"Too shallow on this side for the excursion boat. So we rely on Capitán Picos."

"Terrific." He looked around as if he expected a bellman to appear. "This place looks like a ghost town. Where is everybody?"

"It's siesta time, Rebner. You'll have to be your own bellhop." He would have been on his own at any time. My Bororos were laborers, not valets.

With a wheezy sigh, Rebner bent down and hefted his suitcases. I took the garment bag.

"What's in this thing, Rebner?"

"A suit. In case Montezuma pays us a visit."

"Wrong country."

I noticed he wore a showy Rolex. What next?

We walked from the riverbank into Station Four's utilitarian sparseness. Out of the sun's glare, under the half-dozen tall trees left standing in the cleared rainforest floor, the temperature dropped noticeably.

"Jesus!" Rebner muttered again, this time with vehemence. "Is this all there is to it? A clearing in the jungle?"

"Research lab on the right, mess hut with kitchen and cook's quarters. Storage-generator-and-radio room building up there at the west end. The radio is our only direct contact with the outside. Capitán Picos operates a transceiver at his end. Now over there—"

Obviously not listening, Rebner blundered on ahead.

"You have any idea where you're going?" I pointed at the weather-faded clapboard building to our left. "Living quarters."

He stared at the low, shed-like frame residence with the station's standard corrugated metal roofing.

"Oh, Christ."

"Felicia and I are in the near end. You'll be in the other end. The latrine shed is behind the residence, at the edge of the clearing. There's running water back there when the generator is on, and we have a community spigot just behind the building."

"Latrine?"

"This is a research station, Rebner. Not a resort. At the far end of the residence, you'll find what Felicia calls our 'spa.' Just an open cistern to collect run-off from the residence roof. In the rainy season, it's our bathtub."

We walked toward the residence, Rebner obviously stunned by the elemental level of station facilities.

"These large trees in the compound were left for shade." I was enjoying my role as tour guide for Mr. Numb-With-Shock. "The ones with the scaly red bark are mahogany. The taller ones with spiky trunks and buttress roots are kapoks. Their canopy keeps out direct sun. The place is quite livable. Once you get used to the humidity."

As we neared the bare-essential residence, Rebner said, as if he hadn't listened to a damned word, "Your wife...Felicia? When do I get to meet the little woman?"

That struck me as the patronizing limit. I'd already had it with this Philadelphia philanderer. Not only was I instinctively put off by anyone this much taller than I am, Rebner was a distressing contrast to my sparse frame. My trousers and shirtsleeves flapped around skinny limbs. Rebner, even in his soiled safari rig, managed to project a debonair aura, a triumph of attitude over travel grittiness.

I noticed an intrusively sweet aroma wafting through the musk of rotting vegetation. What could — then I realized Rebner wore designer shaving cologne, still lingering this late in the day.

The little woman, he had said. As if a sad apple like me would attract only the kind of mousy, work-a-day wife that trite phrase intimated. Well, this cocky clod was in for a surprise, wasn't he?

"Felicia will join us for supper," I said. "At the moment, it's siesta time for her, too."

Except for us, the whole station was asleep: Felicia, the stolid Bororo Indians — I had been told they were Bororos, but in a country that encouraged racial intermarriage, it was hard to be precise — and Agata, our housekeeper-cook, a mixed-breed woman I judged to be in her early thirties. The Bororos trotted here daily from their village a few miles downriver. Agata, the best worker of the three, lived here in a room behind the kitchen.

Employer to employee, I showed Rebner to his barren quarters, pointed out the latrine, the water pump—and the screened-off wooden tank that, as I'd said already, served for bathing when the roof's run-off was enough to fill it. Then I left the man to settle in until suppertime.

I hadn't succumbed to the siesta habit. There was always more than enough for me to do in the lab without putting a blank hole in the day.

As I walked across the clearing toward the frame-and-screen lab building, I felt a pang of contriteness. Rebner was no model of geniality, but I hadn't been all that gentlemanly myself. Even so, I was unable to shake the certainty I had felt the minute Rebner stepped ashore.

The rainy season was about to begin, but with Theodore Rebner aboard, I was convinced Station Four faced a problem far more disruptive than sudden rainsqualls.

2

oncentration on my work was impossible. I shoved away my notebook, already thick with handwritten findings. For a long moment, I stood in the doorway of the frame-and-screen lab shed. Then without real purpose, I wandered back to the residence.

"I thought I heard the launch." Felicia looked up from the journal she had begun to keep. "Is he here?"

"He's here."

"Is he what you expected?"

I hunkered down in one of our two camp chairs. "You could say he's more religious than I expected."

"Religious?"

"He says 'Christ' and 'Jesus' a lot."

"Oh, funny, Emmett. Give him a chance. Maybe he'll turn out to be a benefit to the camp."

"You got that half right."

I sat back and watched her scrawl, recalling with amusement my literally running into her during my grad studies at the University of Florida. In the cafeteria line, I had ducked around her to get at the coffee urn. At that instant, she turned away from the counter and—Bang! Her milk carton bounced on the floor.

"Oh, I am so sorry," I blurted. "My fault, my fault."

I picked up the leaking carton, looked for a trash basket. She walked to an empty table. I tossed the ruptured carton, snagged a fresh one.

"Mind if I join you?" I'd noticed she always ate alone. No circle of admirers. In that sense, we were kindred spirits.

She looked startled. "N—no," gestured at the chair across from her.

I settled in, smiled at her. She wasn't pretty. Wasn't ugly, either. An honest, slightly defensive face. A bookworm face, but with possibilities. Don't-give-a-damn hair, randomly brushed, but a nice caramel color. Soft, aqua eyes. Bee-sting breasts behind her men's blue shirt worn tails-out over her bony-hipped Levis.

"Emmett Durkin," I said, reaching across the table to shake her slender hand. "Muddling through my masters in marine bio. You?"

"English lit. Chaucer and such."

"Going to be a teacher?" What the hell else could she do with a major in English lit?

"I don't know what I'm going to be. My father cares more than I do. He wanted me to go to 'Hahvad,' where he went."

"But?"

"He pushed and I applied. But my heart wasn't in it. They detected that up in Cambridge, and I got turned down."

"Oh boy."

"I'll say, 'oh boy.' A grim scene. Then father said, 'Well, you're damn well going to college somewhere.'" She opened the milk container, poured half a glass. "And I said, 'How about here?'"

"You're a Floridian?" I said with some surprise. I'd met hardly any native Floridians in this state of northern refugees.

"No, we're Philadelphians. Down here in the winter. Daddy has a house on Captiva."

"Where's that?"

"It's an island at the northern tip of Sanibel Island. Off Fort Myers. We 'winter there,' as Daddy puts it. 'Warm salt water instead of cold salt slush.'" She sipped her milk. "You?"

"Peoria, Illinois."

She grinned.

"I know, I know. Middle America's most typical city. So they say. And they're right. I hit on marine biology as a sure way out of the grasslands."

And so it went. From the clashed beginning to a comfortable — well — closeness. At the end of the most pleasant meal I'd had at U of F — hell, anywhere — I asked for her phone number. I felt I had found a possible date who wouldn't turn me down. And she didn't. I liked her for that, and I liked her for her intelligence. Trite but true. We became an "item," which titillated only ourselves. Explored Gainesville. In the Toyota her father had loaned her, we took a couple of day trips to St. Augustine and far more rural Cedar Key.

I was close to panicked when her parents insisted on driving up to the college one weekend, obviously to size up this "Emmett" she had been telling them of. Meeting Bert Noonan, I felt like a lowly private meeting General LeMay, including the jutting cigar. I thought Felicia's mother, Sada, was a dead ringer for tart and imperious TV actress Bea

Arthur. The upshot, I felt, shot me down in their eyes, but they did invite us to a weekend on Captiva's narrow and exclusive land spit. For further inspection, in my case. With the Gulf on the west and Pine Island Sound just a few hundred feet on the east, I thought the island was a hell of a place to be in a hurricane. Which was why, in addition to summer's thought-to-be unbearable heat, the Noonans were Captiva snowbirds, arriving in October, departing in May.

I found the weekend visit courteous but distant. Unfortunately, I had no van or von in front of my name and no 2nd or 3rd behind it. Standoff with her family, but no deterrent at all to Felicia. We returned to the University realizing, by God, we were in love! And during a stunningly torrid weekend at remote Lake Okeechobee, I asked her to marry me.

To my surprise as much as hers, she breathed a fervent, "Oh, yes."

The wedding took place after graduation, with Felicia relieved she could slam Chaucer's tome shut forever, with me eager to accept an offer from Mote Marine on Florida's west coast. The Noonans' Philadelphia mansion made their Captiva place look like a beach house—which it was, of course. King Farouk style. I remember "marriage week" as a kaleidoscope of silks, satins and navy blue suits. Felicia was the star. I had a bit part, thank God. A tugboat in a sea of yachts.

My stolid Midwestern parents arrived barely in time for directions to the church.

Slim, grey-haired Dad and short, solidly built Mom were warm to Felicia, wary otherwise. They enjoyed the church's brief Presbyterian ceremony, but the reception back at Chez Noonan left them visibly numb and seeking escape. Us, too. Replacing Felicia's tiring Toyota Corolla, our new Dodge Caravan—a wedding gift from her parents and registered in her name—took us to Atlantic City. "Bermuda?" Bert Noonan had offered. I thanked him, but I felt a father-in-law-financed honeymoon was not my idea of independence. Neither was the Caravan, but at least it was registered as Felicia's. So off to the Jersey coast to honeymoon on my meager savings from my pre-college retail clerking career.

***

Except for the Okeechobee episode, intimacy was new to me. I delighted in its revelations. But Felicia Noonan Durkin turned out to be a not entirely inspired coupler. Religiously adhering to her daily pill schedule, she yielded herself at lengthy intervals, lay there letting me roam over her lean body, facilitated my eagerness with passivity, not passion. At best, she was cooperative, but I was not convinced her little climactic yelp was the real thing. Yet we both were new at this. After a week of not quite intimately finding each other, we drove back to Philadelphia, thence to Florida, a long several day's grind in the Caravan.

Soon my more compelling love was my work at Mote Marine Laboratory, a privately funded marine research facility on Longboat Key, a barrier island off Bradenton and Sarasota. The salary was enough for us to rent a little house in Bradenton's outskirts, but our style of living was far from sumptuous.

***

Six months after our Bradenton arrival, a letter. From the Rebner Foundation in, of all places, Philadelphia. Apparently my progress in Mote's red tide study had attracted attention elsewhere, or so I had thought. I read aloud to Felicia the unexpected job offer from the Foundation chairman, pondered, then looked her straight in the eye. "A coincidence?"

"You mean because it's in Philadelphia?"

"Tell me you had nothing to do with this."

"Emmett, I learned about it just this moment."

"You think your father has an in with—" I glanced back at the letter— "Oliver Rebner?"

"He knows him, yes. In fact, Daddy is on the Foundation board."

I wasn't all that pleased by my suspicion that Daddy's hand was in this somehow. But my curiosity pigeon-holed that mild resentment. So I took a sick-leave day and winged off to Philadelphia.

***

"What an opportunity!" I burst out when I dashed from the debarking crowd at Southwest International Airport after returning from my interview. I threw my arms around Felicia. "Oliver—he insists on first names—asked me to run the Foundation's marine research station in Brazil!"

She struggled free and gasped, "Rio, I hope? Or at least São Paulo."

I picked up my carry-on bag and we walked toward the escalators. "Actually, it's up the mysterious, exotic Amazon."

"Oh. God, Emmett. How far up?"

"Several hundred miles, I'm told." My elation began to fade. This was going to be a selling job. "It's a hell of a career boost. Pure on-site research. We'll be replacing the current station chief."

"Why is he leaving?"

I followed her onto the descending escalator steps. "It's only a two-year assignment, Felicia." That was true enough. What I didn't add was—if I interpreted Oliver Rebner's wordy circumlocution accurately—Dr. Sidney Warnowski, the current station chief, had become a burnout after thirteen months.

"Two years in the jungle," Felicia murmured.

"That's all. Then with that behind us, there's going to be no limit to where we can go from there. Surely, a book—even two books. One of them written by you, Felicia. On your life in the rain forest."

We walked across the ramp toward the parking garage. "Emmett," she said, "I couldn't write a book."

"Of course you can. That English major—"

"It was English literature, not jungle reportage."

"You can do it. I know you can, and with two years' experience on the Trombetas—

"Trombetas? What's that?"

Finally a spark of interest.

"That's where Research Station Four is. It's a tributary of the Amazon River. Really quite beautiful, Oliver said."

Oliver Rebner had said no such thing, but Felicia needed reinforcement, and surely anywhere in lush Amazon country must have some attractive aspects.

"Well..." Long pause. "Maybe I can find something there to like," she muttered as we walked into the parking garage.

Not exactly a ringing endorsement. "It will be something we'll always remember," I assured her.

"That's what I'm afraid of." She handed me the keys to the Caravan.

Unenthusiastic acquiescence was her often-standard response. The best I could expect, I decided, from a woman born into Quaker City society. In fact, I had been surprised she had agreed to marry me, given her parents' stiffly correct bearing, unrelenting from our first meeting. I suspected Bert Noonan had never considered mousy Felicia's marriage prospects particularly bright. Our union, I assumed, was viewed by Bert and Sada as a degree or two better than spinsterhood for daughter Felicia. How glowing could be the prospects for me, her bookish science nerd?

To his credit, though, Bert refrained from insultingly subsidizing my modest Mote Marine earnings. But had he stuck a finger in the Rebner Foundation's offer? Improbable, I told myself. The salary uptick was impressive, but would a concerned father exile his daughter into the Amazon rain forest as a means of getting her husband a pay raise?

However it had come about, I was elated at the career enhancement potential— and by the prospect of the work itself. I gave Mote Marine notice, and one year after the date of our marriage, Felicia and I found ourselves up the Amazon, 500 miles from Brazil's northeast coast.

"And a thousand miles from Rio," she had muttered when Capitán Picos's asthmatic steamboat bumped us ashore. After a glance around the small clearing, she grumped, "My God, Emmett, this place doesn't come close to the standards of the cheapest Pocono Mountain summer camp!"

We were greeted with a surprisingly warm pantomime by Station Four's two Bororo Indian day workers, Jheem the tall one, and Haree, short and dumpy. Their names, I eventually deduced, had been given them by a now-defunct bootleg teak operation some miles upriver. Both sported what my father called "bowl haircuts," presumably accomplished by placing a bowl on the head then trimming around its inverted rim. Each nightfall, Jheem and Haree had the good sense to return to their own probably more comfortable village a mile to the north. Its access was a rank path I never had the slightest impulse to explore.

I replaced a tattered, scraggly-bearded skeleton named Sid Warnowski, a wreck of a Doctor of Marine Science, who had been sent here by the Foundation just over a year ago. His specialty was supposed to have been the fresh water stingray, but observation told me it more recently was the 100-proof pinch bottle. Warnowski hadn't made it much more than halfway through his two-year contractual hitch.

As I helped him bumble aboard the launch, he muttered, "It's the isolation. The goddam isolation. You'll find out. You're doomed, man, you and your missus. You just don't know it yet."

That had shaken me, but I realized the outburst was that of a man in alcohol-fueled delirium. Then he gasped, "Indy. You take care of Indy."

What in hell did that mean? Or was it only the fuzzy mutter of a demented man?

After the launch huffed out of sight around the south bend with Warnowski hunched in its stern, we found a quarter-full bottle of Haig & Haig behind the tattered linens in the residence cupboard. I poured the booze onto the spongy ground behind the building.

Warnowski's two Bororos and his housekeeper had quit a week ago, she huffing away via Picos's launch. I'd been told by phone from Oliver she had reached her limits of tolerance for the drunken doctor's verbal abuse. Word of his departure brought the two Indians back, but after their courteous greeting, they were wary until they realized it wasn't in either of us to be anything but civil. The Indians thereafter became as dependable as the most conscientious of white-collar nine-to-fivers.

Warnowski's housekeeper, we realized after a few days of domestic drudgery, had fled for good. So for some months, the Bororos brought with them a woman from their village who tried her best to cook and clean. But she was capable of only the simplest dishes, many with unfathomable contents. And she understood not one word of English. When I mentioned the situation to Capitán Pecos, he nodded with great enthusiasm. "I know of a señora who might…si, she just might."

On his next trip, Agata was aboard. An experienced restaurant cook, she was willing also to handle general housekeeping—and she spoke adequate English. Something in her cocoa-brown eyes, though, made me hesitate.

"Something…"

"Oh, don't be ridiculous!" Felicia scoffed. "Hire the woman."

One sunny morning two weeks after we arrived, Felicia stepped from our residence room's back door and stopped short. "Yow!" she cried, staring at something on the ground a few yards away.

I rushed out. She pointed at an eight-foot-long, glossy, blue-black snake. "God, Emmett!"

The snake gazed up at us then slithered into the forest understory behind the latrine. Quite casually, I thought.

"It's an indigo, Felicia. Harmless. In Florida they drape indigos over tourists' shoulders for photos to chill the home folks."

Indigo... I pondered. "Indy," Warnowski had said. "Take care of Indy." Was it possible the poor bastard had only an eight-foot snake for a friend? A broken man concerned only for his pet snake?

"I think we just met Indy, Felicia. Now our welcome is complete."

Thereafter, Indy appeared fairly often, eyeing Felicia or me for long moments, then calmly undulating back to the Station's undergrowth boundary. We respected his right to be here.

***

Now, a year in exile had inevitably changed us both, but Felicia most remarkably. Preoccupied with my work, I had become sun-browned and sinewy with my careless attire hanging loose. Felicia, through Agata's culinary temptations, possibly augmented by some magical jungle aura, had blossomed like a tropical flower. Her bony hips filled out. Her flattish little breasts ripened to lush prominence. Like a neglected bud unfolding into an exotic bloom, she projected an ambience of sweet enticement.

I was elated by her metamorphosis into a stunningly compelling woman. I thrilled to her now-eager embrace, her newfound urgency for gratification. I was a hungry man at an exotic banquet. I couldn't get enough. I began to desert the lab for sexually experimental siestas. I woke listless from nocturnal pleasures I had never imagined Felicia would dare initiate. I was overwhelmed by her uninhibited passion, drunk with it. Drunk...

"It's the goddam isolation..."

In less than a year, the bottle had ruined Warnowski. In a comparable time, I was neglecting my research for something even more addictive. This had to stop. Pleading the demand of my work, I begged off from our siesta tumbles and cut our nighttime calisthenics to a more restful frequency.

She pouted like a schoolgirl. "You don't love me anymore."

"Of course I love you, Felicia. But I just can't neglect my work any longer."

She came to me that night, and I succumbed all too readily. This was not going to be easy. Ultimately, I managed to have her settle for a lot less intimacy than I knew she now craved. Less than I wanted, too. But I was getting some work done.

She set about learning a working knowledge of Portuguese, with Agata as her tutor. Next, she had a fling at writing a book of our lives here, as I had suggested. But her interest soon flagged in her day-to-day boredom. In a carry-over from her prep school days, she decided to take up archery. I had Capitán Picos order then transport upriver a thirty-pound-pull longbow, two dozen brass-tipped target arrows and a three-foot straw-backed target. With hours to kill, Felicia became a surprisingly proficient archer. But in the rain forest's unremitting monotony, that pastime too faded. The bow and quiver of arrows hung on our residence wall, now a part of the rustic décor.

She was a bright woman, and I tried to interest her in the lab work. Maybe she could develop into a worthy lab assistant. But she hated the "disgusting squirmy things" I found so absorbing. Now she spent most of her days in our barebones residence, reading and rereading the lurid adventure paperbacks Sid Warnowski had left behind. These were augmented by English-language novels Capitán Pecos periodically boated in from the limited bookstalls of rural Oriximiná.

For me, everything had fallen comfortably into place. Now the heavy hand of benevolent nepotism in distant Philadelphia threatened to screw it up. Fresh from what Oliver had described in his letter as "a little social setback" had come obviously unrepentant nephew Theodore Rebner.

3

The man from Philadelphia's casual amble into the mess hut was marred by his tripping over the doorsill as he scanned the table.

"Am I late?"

Agata, her ebony hair in a thick braid down her back, had already served the fish soup. Tall but shapeless in her ankle-length gray caftan, her only spot of color was a half-dollar size, rough-cut green stone suspended on a thin silver chain around her neck. Felicia herself wore nothing more decorative than eggshell cotton slacks and a plain white T-shirt—which, I was suddenly aware, focused Rebner's attention on her lush bustline.

"Your seat's over here, Rebner."

"I thought in South America everybody ate late." He plunked down on the camp chair.

"We eat early to reduce the need to be outside after dark." I turned to Felicia. "This is Theodore Rebner. Rebner, my wife, Felicia."

He bowed in her direction. "Pretty name for a lovely woman. So this is the missus. Well, well, well. A pleasure to meet you, Mrs. Durkin."

"Felicia, please, Mr. Rebner."

"And I will be most happy if you would call me Ted."

He had undergone a transition from his riverside boorishness to smooth civility.

"The menu tonight?" Ted asked her.

"Fish broth and..." she spoke with hovering Agata in proud Portuguese, then turned back to Ted... "Roast pork and manioc. With papaya for dessert."

"Impressive, here in the middle of nothing at all."

Felicia smiled at the compliment, obviously enjoying her unaccustomed role as gracious hostess. "Agata is from Manaus. She was a chef's assistant at the Restaurante La Barca there. We're very fortunate."

The delicious aroma of roast pork loin, carved from a wild boar the two Indian men had speared in honor of the occasion, provided an illusion of civilization in the raw hut. It was abruptly shattered by a hair-rippling screech.

"What in Christ's name is that?" Ted burst out.

"Jaguar, getting ready for the evening hunt. They pretty much stay clear of us." I said that by reflex. I had just realized something a lot more disturbing than a jaguar's evening scream. Since Teddy boy strode into the mess hut, the man's speculative slate-blue gaze had not wavered from Felicia — until the jaguar's shriek split the compound's silence.

Two predators now?

"Shoulda done what I wanted to do," Ted muttered.

Felicia peered at him with raised eyebrows. "What you wanted to do?"

"Act. On Broadway." Up went that chin. "In fact, I auditioned for 'Dangerous Assumption.'"

Felicia looked starry-eyed. "And?"

"No acting lessons, no training, but they told me I was a natural."

"Did you get the part?"

"Not the one I was after. Not the lead."

"What part did you get?" She sounded breathless.

"They offered me the role of some damned servant. I told them to go to hell and I walked out."

Exit pouting, I thought, straight into the arms of Uncle Oliver, who decided to straighten out this hollow-head with a rainforest sojourn at isolated Station Four.

"I'm so sorry," Felicia said. "Didn't you try again?"

"They wouldn't recognize talent if it fell on them."

"Breakfast at seven," I said. "In the lab at seven-thirty." I couldn't resist a little smile. "I'll teach you what I can."

***

Ted was not a morning person. At breakfast, he met my "Good morning" with no more than a surly nod. In silence, our Philadelphia clotheshorse — white ducks and a tan Ralph Lauren polo shirt today — downed his canned orange juice, powdered eggs scrambled and thick-cut bacon. In an apparent effort to jolt himself fully awake, he tossed back two cups of Agata's excellent Arabica coffee. Then he leaned back in his camp chair, gazed up at the raw lumber underside of the roof. And stared.

"My God, there's something live up there."

"A few good-luck geckos. We stay in our part of this little world, they stay in theirs." I glanced at my watch. "Time to get to work...Ted."

The corrugated metal roof of the research building — well, glorified shed — protected a work counter, sink, cupboard, microscope, manual typewriter and several filing cabinets at the entrance end. The rest of the large interior was occupied by four rows of bubbling aquariums: a row along each frame-and-screen sidewall, two rows back-to-back down the center. The most permanent part of the structure was the concrete floor slab.

"The power in here and in the other buildings is from a gas-fueled generator at the upper end of the compound." I slipped into lecture mode. "The generator also powers the water pumps in the kitchen and at the residence, plus the radio equipment up there at the north end of the generator-storage building. To conserve fuel, I've timed the generator to run at intervals. That requires..."

"So that was the thrum-thrum I heard cut out just after dark, then back on again too damned early this morning."

I pressed on. "...that requires the aquarium pumps to run from those storage batteries you see under the aquarium benches during 'off' intervals. After you're here awhile, you won't notice the generator noise."

I stepped between the rows of bubbling tanks to our right. "Now in this first..."

"Felicia doesn't join us for breakfast?"

"Seven's too early for her." To focus his wandering attention, I tapped my forefinger on the edge of the large murky tank. "In this first aquarium..."

With his back to me, he scanned the work counter. "What's that little metal box with the red bulb on top?"

"That's a receiver that tells me Capitán Picos is calling me on the radio up in the storage building. You might have seen the little antenna on the roof above the door. And the bigger one on the north end of the storage building."

"So the light here goes on and you go up there? Why don't you have the radio down here?"

"Too much heat and far too much humidity. Up there, a not so great but adequate air conditioner manages to cool the room somewhat and dehumidify it when the generator runs. Because of atmospherics and the radio's less-than-prime condition, I can depend on it only as far as Oriximiná. Picos has his set up in his home office. It's not exactly an A-one set-up, but it can be our lifeline."

"Jesus."

I tapped the tank again. "As I was saying, Ted, in this first aquarium is a truly impressive specimen of Electophorus electricus. Note these two wires leading to the voltmeter on the side of the tank. Their purpose..."

"Wait a minute...Emmett. In English, okay? Electro-for-what?"

"I thought the technical name was self-sufficient, along with your keen visual observation."

"Looks like a big fat water snake to me."

"That is an Amazon electric eel, capable of repeated discharges as high as six hundred volts. Enough to stun a horse. And kill a man."

"Why him?"

"I don't follow you, Ted."

"What are you doing with this thing?"

At least that crude question showed a flicker of interest. "I'm tabulating precise measurements of its discharge rates, voltage peaks and its total output capability."

He shrugged. "Why?"

"There could be medical, even military applications," I told him with a degree of satisfaction. "Next, we have three tanks of Sphaeroides annulatus."

"Uh-huh. Look like fish to me."

"They are fish. Not native here, they're west-coast Gulf puffers. Saltwater fish, but the Foundation has no facility in that area, so they're here — and it's a challenge to maintain the proper salinity. Their flesh is edible, even delicious. But the intestines, liver, gonads and skin contain tetrodotoxin, a deadly poison."

I glanced at my superfluous "assistant" and was gratified by his look of revulsion.

"The victim first notices tingling of the lips and tongue," I went on with a degree of relish at his finicky little scowl. "That develops into numbness of the entire body, respiratory difficulty, sometimes hemorrhages in the skin, muscle twitches, tremors then convulsions. There's no antidote and only a forty-percent survival rate. The Foundation is interested in the puffer's pharmacological possibilities."

"Swell."

We moved on to an outsized tank of brownish water, its sandy floor paved with large fleshy discs.

"Stingrays," Ted offered, to my surprise.

"Potamotrygon motoro, the Amazon variety of the freshwater stingray. The venomous barb on this species is located well out on the tail instead of at its base."

"So?"

"So that weapon near the end of the long whip of a tail makes Potamotrygon among the most dangerous of the stingrays. The wound is hugely painful, of course, and attacks in the upper body have been fatal. Again, there is no specific antivenin."

He bent to peer into the tank, shrugged and straightened. I waited for the obvious question, but Ted said nothing.

"If you are wondering about the purpose of the rays' being here — "which he apparently wasn't — "it's for the extraction of venom for shipment to a Miami medical lab in search of a quick-acting antidote."

Sweat had begun to stain his polo shirt, though not from the impact of my little hall of aquatic terrors, I decided. The man appeared totally disinterested in the station's purpose. He was sweating from the ever-present humidity that hung over our compound like invisible steam.

"Christ," Ted muttered. "I had to get here in the hot season."

"It's always the hot-and-humid season here. We're only a couple hundred miles south of the equator." I stopped at a covered aquarium in which crouched a half-dozen bright yellow frogs. "Here we have Phyllobates terribilis."

"Sounds like fun," he said tonelessly.

"No fun involved. Rubber gloves for handling these beauties, and we burn the gloves afterwards. Each of these specimens exudes enough neurotoxin on its skin to kill everyone here. You've heard of blowguns, I presume. The Indians use the secretion of these frogs for blowgun dart poison."

Ted gazed through the aquarium's protective glass lid, but his air of detached boredom was beginning to infuriate me. We rounded the end of the rows and started up the other side.

"Now," I said, still relishing the lecture mode, "we come to Urinophilus erythrurus, members of the catfish family known locally as 'candirú.'" I crouched to point out the several dozen matchstick-size catfish hovering near the bottom of the tank. "These little devils are one of the most fascinating of all dangerous marine animals. From the scientific name, you can deduce that they avidly seek out the victim's urethra…"

I looked up from my crouch. Ted wasn't listening. His attention was riveted through the screening to the woman ambling across the compound toward the mess hut. Buxom in a frilly cream blouse, sky-blue skirt swirling about her legs. Felicia on her way to breakfast. Now dressed for the Ritz.

"Ted? Ted!"

"Yeah, what?"

The man was insufferable. "Your first duty is to take that broom over there and sweep this place clean." Agata would be happy to be relieved of her lab-cleaning stints. Dynamic balance, since she was now cooking for another mouth.

"Sweep?"

"Yes, sweep. After you finish back here, report to me up front. There are housekeeping opportunities up there as well. I'm afraid I left the sink in a mess yesterday."

For the moment, that should take care of Teddy the Unready. I strode back to the work counter satisfied I had properly fitted the man into his place in the scheme of things. At the bottom.

***

With Felicia joining us for lunch, Ted appeared newly energized.

"Quite a chamber of horrors hubby has out there." He nodded over his shoulder in the direction of the lab. "Convinced me never to play with his aquarium collections."

At least I'd made some small inroad into that pudding brain. But I surely did not appreciate his eyes centering on Felicia alone.

"How do you stand it, a vibrant woman like you, stuck out here in this jungle camp?"

"You haven't seen the majestic beauty of the river, the stateliness of the kapoks and teaks..." She grinned impishly. "I read a lot, Ted. And I'm doing some sketching."

"Uncle Oliver told me you're from Philadelphia."

"Near Bala Cynwyd. And I went to The Collingdale School up near Allentown. There were a lot of prominent Philadelphians there."

"Collingdale?" Ted asked. "Did you know the Carterets?"

"The Huntingdon Valley Carterets? Sissie was in my class!"

And they were off. Old Home Week for preppies, with me, a lowly Peoria High grad, excluded. Why couldn't Teddy Boy have come from Cleveland or, better yet, some remote burg like Boise?

"Back to work," I grumped when they had chattered as far as a spring cotillion they had coincidentally attended at the Belleview Hotel five years ago. Agata slipped into view to clear away the remains of her version of caldeirada, a fish stew thickened with farina and livened up with a peppery sauce. As she piled up our dishes, I caught her flicker of a frown at Ted then an eyebrow-raised glance at me.

"You can give the Bororos a hand up at the generator shack," I told him. "They're replacing rotting siding with boards from our lumber stockpile up there." I hoped a little manual labor would damp him down a bit.

"I don't speak Bororo."

"Neither do I, but they know enough English to get things done. Don't underestimate them. They're good people."

At 2:30, I stepped to the lab doorway to take a look up there. The two Indian men, near naked in their leather loincloths, worked alone.

I found Teddy in the shade behind the residence, sprawled in a camp chair, his hand wrapped around a glass of lemonade. That was irritating enough. Worse was finding Felicia seated back there with him.

"Damn it, Ted. I told you..."

"Enough's enough in this damned heat, professor. Anyway, seems to me we have a minimum to do, and all the time in the world to do it."

"The Foundation gave me explicit instructions..."

"Oh, Emmett," Felicia broke in, "it's his first day. Besides, I haven't had anyone from the outside world to talk to since we came here."

And in all that time, no one here had ever defied me. "Felicia..."

She had turned back to Ted, her eyes ablaze with new-found interest. "The Elmo Turners. Did you know them too?"

An ugly confrontation at this point would erase any hope of maneuvering Teddy into usefulness. I swallowed sour fury and strode away, fighting my impulse to yank the arrogant bastard out of his chair and pop him one on his pretty-boy jaw.

***

That night at supper, Ted snorted, "Fish again?" as if the chef at this resort had lost all culinary imagination.

I struggled to keep my voice from spiraling into an angry shout. "I'm afraid the nearest supermarket is several hundred miles out of reach."

The one-sided dinner talk returned to the Keystone State's southeastern environs and the rumored peccadillos of certain otherwise stalwart citizens.

As Felicia and I prepared for bed, I found myself still stressed. "That clown has no interest whatever in what we're doing here—or anything else I can discern—excluding social frolic. No wonder Uncle Oliver exiled him out of Philadelphia.... Hell, out of the northern hemisphere."

Brushing her shoulder-length flow of golden hair, she paused. "Oh, Emmett, back off a little. He's amusing in a way. He calls the Bororos Curly and Larry, both with Moe's hairdo. And he thinks Agata..."

"Felicia, I really don't want to hear any disparaging comments on our staff."

In the dim light from our 40-watt overhead bulb, I noticed her eyes were more alive than I'd seen them in months. My heart stuttered.

"And he's brought all the Main Line gossip. Including so many people I know."

She slipped under her cot's mosquito netting.

"Including the little incident your friend wrote you about—the one that got him thrown out of town?"

"Well, that may have been as much her doing as his. Such things are never totally one-sided."

I reached up to switch off the light. "You're defending the man."

"I'm being impartial. Go to sleep."

4

S leepless beneath the tented mosquito netting, I thought back to the interview in the Rebner Foundation's Broad Street offices. I flew from Southwest Florida's sub-tropical breezes to Pennsylvania's chilling autumn gusts and took a taxi from Philadelphia International. I was grateful for the cab's smoky warmth; I hadn't thought to bring an overcoat. In perpetually mild Southwest Florida, I didn't even own an overcoat.

The Foundation's fifth-floor headquarters were an intimidating suite of polished walnut, thick carpeting and muffled efficiency. Foundation President Oliver Rebner occupied corner acreage with expansive views of both Broad and Market Streets. I was ushered into this power center by a meek woman with dingy hair in a ponytail tied with what looked like a shoestring.

Rebner, a bald-domed, imposing mound of a man in banker's blue, glanced up from his paper-laden desk. I assumed his blue-and-gray striped tie proclaimed he was an alumnus of some prestigious prep school.

"Mr. Durkin," Rebner rumbled as he rose to offer a brief handshake. "Sit yourself down." I took the armless chair in front of the desk, uncomfortable seating no doubt meant to be occupied briefly. I already felt out of place here in my flight-rumpled khaki slacks, tan corduroy jacket, and tightly knotted olive tie. Overdressed attire for Southwest Florida, but up here I felt like sneakers at a board meeting.

"Nice flight?" Rebner asked without any sign of expecting a response. "Let's get down to business." He picked up two stapled sheets I recognized as my résumé. "High school in Peoria, your hometown. Good record there got you a scholarship at the University of Chicago. Which, by the way, I regard as an often underrated but highly pragmatic institution. Earned your masters at the University of Florida. Then to work in Sarasota."

He folded chunky hands on the desk's blotter pad. "Tell me, Durkin, what is your primary interest area with Mote Marine?"

"Red tides, sir. What causes them, and is control possible."

"Red tides." Rebner settled back in his leather chair. "Ever done any work with dangerous marine animals?"

"Not as a primary subject area. About the only such fauna in Florida waters — outside of sharks and stingrays — are the Joubin's octopus, cone shells, and several puffer species. Then, of course, there are the toxins ingested by eating contaminated shellfish, and the..."

He waved an impatient hand. "Why haven't you pursued a doctorate?"

"I plan to work on that after I've had a bit more field experience."

"Interesting, in view of your generation's passion for an unbroken chain of ever higher education. Tell me, Durkin, are you available to serve, say, a two-year stint outside the country? You are a married man. Felicia Noonan. Fine old Philadelphia family, the Noonans. Know them well."

There it had been, I realized, as I stared into the grayness beyond the mosquito netting. The connection.

Rebner then reeled off the Foundation's six research stations, scattered around the globe. Research, he went on, aimed at the medical and possibly military uses of dangerous marine biota. He finished his presentation with the responsibilities of Foundation station chiefs. My God, I realized, he's offering me a station chief position.

"Not a glamorous assignment, Mr. Durkin. Hard work under primitive conditions that are about to cost us the current chief of Station Four. Sid Warnowski has become... Well, it's not an easy responsibility, but the work itself should be compelling. Interested?"

Oliver Rebner rolled on without waiting for a response. "You will be relieving Dr. Warnowski. I'm afraid Sid hasn't lived up to our expectations." From that point, Rebner's conversation was a detailed description of Station Four's remote location, its meager facilities and the Foundation's expectations from its work.

When he paused for breath, I asked him, "What, sir, exactly, does the Foundation do with the, uh, materials sent in by the research stations?"

"Classified."

"Military stuff? Medical?"

"You don't have to concern yourself with that. Your job will be to acquire the... 'stuff,' as you put it. Now, as I said,..." and he reviewed his description of Station Four's facilities. But he wrapped up that unglamorous presentation with a fancy ribbon: a salary offer four times my pay at Mote Marine. My questions evaporated. Sold!

Now, as I twitched, sleepless, on my creaky cot, I was struck with a depressing possibility. Had Uncle Oliver selected me for my scientific promise? As a station chief compliant enough to put up with his useless nephew? Or...

What exactly was the Foundation up to?

Through the following week, I assigned Ted to a succession of minor tasks, which he performed at his lackadaisical leisure—or not at all. One such balk involved the mealworms in a covered tray in a corner of the lab. I propagated the worms as food, primarily for the tree frogs.

"Damned if I'll touch those vile things," Ted announced, and he strode out of the building.

"You'll do as I say!" I shouted after him, but he walked on as if I'd said nothing at all. A half hour later, I spotted him and Felicia strolling along the riverbank.

"Let me give you a thumbnail evaluation, Ted," I said at supper. "So far, you are a negative factor in the work of your uncle's Foundation."

"But here I am, chief. And Uncle Oliver says here I stay. For a whole goddam year." His smile had begun as one of mirth at my impotent comment. Now it was one of mockery.

That night, after a long silence in the darkness of the residence, I said quietly, "He's trouble, Felicia, and you're...not helping."

From her side of our muggy room, I heard nothing.

"Felicia? Are you awake?"

Silence. Then I felt her weight on the edge of my cot.

"He's just a big boy in a man's body, Emmett," she murmured. "Try to understand him."

"I do understand him. That's why I'm so...so pissed."

She brushed the mosquito netting aside and nestled beside me. Minus her pajama bottoms. "He amuses me, but you're my husband."

Which struck me as a peculiar way to put it. Not an affirmation of love; a justification of impropriety.

She slipped under the sheet. A few moments later, I realized she had regressed from a woman eagerly torrid to one of tepid obligation.

***

Ted's respect for items mechanical, I discovered, was on a par with his interest in marine research. The seventeen-foot Boston Whaler Montauk had been provided to the station for specimen gathering. When Felicia and I arrived, I used the Whaler extensively to replenish several of the specimens Warnowski had let die off through drunken neglect. Now, with the lab well stocked, the Whaler sat generally idle. Its cover kept the rain out, but the battery's power slowly drained. Occasionally, I took the boat on recharging runs.

Perhaps Ted might be assigned that not-very-demanding task.

At breakfast one suitably calm and bright morning, I announced, "We'll be taking the Whaler out right after we've eaten, Ted. A short run to keep the battery up."

"Oh, goody!" he mocked. "We're going for a boat ride."

"Ted!" Felicia said with a disarming smile. "Be nice."

"Yeah, okay. At least it'll beat playing janitor for catfish and stingrays."

My Igor actually remembers two of the species, I marveled. A scintilla of progress. "On the dock in fifteen minutes. No need to wear a yachting ensemble. But you'll want to cover your head against the sun."

"Yes, Dad."

I ignored that and turned to Felicia. "Would you like to come along?"

"Thanks, but I'll pass. You know how the sun bouncing off the water affects me. I burn too easily."

I finished my coffee and pushed back from the table. "I'll check the fuel tanks. See you in a few minutes, Ted."

I loosened the cover ties, pulled the big plastic tarp off the boat, folded it and placed it on the dock near our faded-green-paint canoe. Checked the two under-seat fuel tanks. Nearly full. Pulled the key out of my pocket, stuck it in the ignition lock on the console's panel and slipped the power cut-off safety clip in place.

Only four minutes late, Ted clumped down the bank and onto the dock. He wore a gray baseball cap with the bill to the rear.

"You ever been on a power boat before, Ted?"

"Only yachts."

I sidestepped that. "Okay then, follow me through on this. Key's already in the ignition. Before the outboard's fired up, the prop goes in the water. This switch, on the throttle arm." I pressed it and the upraised 90-horse Johnson swung downward with a metallic whine, putting its propeller in the water.

"All right. Throttle in neutral. Ignition—" I twisted the key—"on."

The seldom-used engine kicked over with a clatter. Fired once. Wheezed. Caught. A billowing cloud of blue smoke burst from the exhaust, ballooned up the bank and filtered into the compound.

"Untie bow and stern lines."

"Aye, aye," Ted said sourly and moved with a deficit of alacrity.

"Now we advance the throttle slowly. That shifts us from neutral into drive. And we're off."

Side-by-side on the bench seat behind the midship console, we glided from the dock, afloat on a river of glass.

"What's the range of this thing?" Ted wondered as I swung us northward close to shore.

"I'd guess about forty to fifty miles one-way." I was surprised at his interest. "Planning a trip?"

Could he be thinking of an "escape" run to Oriximiná? It would be almost worth losing the boat to be rid of him. With luck, Picos might even recover it and tow it back here behind his launch.

"You always poop along like this? Is walking speed tops for this tub?"

"This is fast enough to charge the battery, slow enough to conserve fuel. You didn't see a gas pump back there at the station. We have to fill gas cans from the fuel drums behind the storage building then lug them down to the boat. All that puts a damper on wasting fuel for thrills."

Aside from this aggravation beside me, I found our leisurely cruise a welcome escape from the station's tensions. The water was smooth. The morning carried that familiar tang of jungle flora and decay. The air was so clear the miles-distant east shoreline looked deceptively close.

"We're going upstream," I pointed out. "I always head upstream."

"Why?" Ted yipped over the engine's burble.

"If the engine quits, the boat will drift back toward the station. There's a paddle aft, so if…"

"How about showing me what this baby can do?"

Had he listened to a word I'd said? "I told you, this is the optimum sp…"

"Oh, piss on that!" Ted reached over, knocked my hand aside and rammed the throttle full forward.

The engine howled. The Whaler's stern dug in. We were thrown against the seatback. The console's bottom-hinged access door flew open, smacked my shins. The little boat's bow heaved out of the water, crashed back down to cleave a boiling wake.

I clawed forward, slammed Ted's hand free. Yanked the throttle back to slow cruise.

"That does it, you idiot! You just flunked your driving test."

Unperturbed, Ted cried, "Damn! I'll bet we hit fifty. Who'da thunk this tub had that in her?"

I swung the Whaler through a stately 180-degree reverse. A few minutes later, we rounded the bend north of the station. Without another word, I eased the boat to the dock. I damned well would never entrust the Whaler to Captain Kid.

***

As if in retaliation to my reaction to his boating behavior, Ted's infatuation with Felicia became more blatant. At mealtimes, he spoke only to her. During the day, I seldom saw her without him. I seethed in silence.

Until I couldn't hold back another damned minute. "I hope you won't forget," I reminded him in the lab a few days after our boating fiasco, "Felicia is my wife."

But as I said that, I realized how ludicrous it must sound to this hulking playboy. If I were the towering 200-pounder in this scenario and had snarled, "She is my wife!" at a 145-pound Ted Rebner, it would have come off as dramatic. But I realized too late the tableau of Ted looming over me as I squawked up at him made my implied threat almost comical.

He grinned down at me. "Five-foot-six ain't impressive, chief."

"Jimmy Doolittle was five-four," I snarled. "That worked out all right."

"Joseph Stalin was five-four," he shot back. "That worked out all wrong."

"I'm surprised you know who Stalin was," I muttered.

Ted grinned. Water off this lame duck's back. "Hey, listen, I'm not going to sweep, saw or sort worms. Time for a day off. The power boat's off-limits, but mind if I borrow the canoe?"

"Yes, I do mind."

"Thought you would," he said amiably and walked out.

"Come back here!" I fumed. Then I got hold of myself. Another minute or so, and Ted would have me shaking my finger and stamping my foot. Maybe the best way to handle all this was to live and let live. Surely, I could trust Felicia to... Trust her not to... Hadn't she called him a mere boy?

I went about my lab work with more equanimity than I had felt for days. When Ted had not reappeared by lunchtime, I didn't find that disturbing. With luck, the man had fallen out of the canoe and piranhas had picked him to the bone, though I had never seen a trace of those aggressive little scavengers in this vicinity.

When Felicia also failed to appear at the mess hut for lunch, I decided to take a not-so-casual stroll along the riverbank. As I reached its crest, I spotted the two of them hauling the canoe up on the floating dock.

I stepped back so the edge of the bank hid me from their view. The man had me spying on my own wife. Then my guilt became anger. Felicia's bright sundress — where had that come from? — had merged with Ted's suntans. They were acting a hell of a lot more than casually friendly down there. And they both looked flushed and, well, raggedy. From lifting the canoe onto the dock? Or...

Live and let live? Through an almost unbearable lunch, I was assailed by waves of fury, frustration and disillusionment. With Felicia. With myself.

Ted Rebner, an inferior example of manhood, and my own wife, whose intellect had captivated me in the first place, showed signs of more than infatuation. The man was of no use to Station Four. And I had absolutely no use for him.

I was convinced he threatened our marriage.

5

With a length of wooden dowel, I agitated the Electrophorus eel, glanced at the volt-meter, plopped down on the lab stool, opened my notebook — and drew a blank. I couldn't recall the damned volt reading.

My mind was not on lab work. Not on anything here. Not wandering but acutely focused decades ago — on my years in grade school. Specifically on one Frank Tuffare, known to all as Tuffy. The nickname had shaped him, probably since kindergarten. By the time he entered my sixth grade class, he had developed bullying to a fine art, and I became his target of choice. I was skinny and small. He was lumpy and tall. No imagination. Just juvenile taunts, challenges no one dared call him on. And sometimes, when his audience was big enough, a clout or two. I never clouted him back. Should have but never did. I finished my last two years there in frustration and self-disgust.

The same damned state in which I now found myself. Ted Rebner was Tuffy Tuffare grown up physically, but atrophied in attitude.

To my great relief, the Tuffares moved to Chicago the year I entered Peoria High. But my miserable memories lived on a while, as did the disparaging nickname he had given me, Turkey. "Here he is, folks, Turkey Durkin. Ta Da!" as I slunked to my desk or fumbled at recess catch-game efforts. As I confided to Felicia one night of intimate secrets, I didn't shake that hateful nickname until I entered college.

Tuffy Tuffare then, Ted Rebner now. And I found myself in the same state of frustrated despair. I lay down my ballpoint Bic and stared into the compound. God, I'd failed myself then. Damned if I'd do it all over again! I was the station chief, the man in charge. But how did I handle this mess?

***

"So, Emmett," Felicia said at supper a little too brightly, "how was your day?"

I still could picture her and Ted, steamy and rumpled, down on the dock this afternoon. A canoe, of all places. How could you, Felicia?

"Emmett?"

"My day," I said after what I realized had been a disturbingly long silence, "was one of profound disillusion."

Ted grinned. "Something went wrong in your little world of weirdos?"

"That's one way of putting it, Ted." My voice was ice. I swirled the dregs of my coffee, then met his insolent gaze. "You will report to the lab immediately after breakfast tomorrow. Be ready to put in a full day's work."

Ted's smirk didn't waver. "Pass me the bread."

***

After breakfast the following morning, he didn't appear at the lab. Blatantly visible from the lab, he sunbathed bare-chested in shorts on a rusty folding lounge chair in front of the residence. Then he stepped back to his room to emerge in khaki slacks and blue T. Strolled aimlessly around the compound, avoiding the lab building. For several hours, he disappeared. And, I noted, so did Felicia. I refused to lower myself further by searching for them.

In the days that followed, those prolonged absences became routine. And the behavior of the Indian laborers changed. Until now, even when they were hard at work and I approached, they managed to face me respectfully until I nodded and passed by. Now, except when I directly addressed them, I found myself ignored.

Agata had been less subservient than they, but she had managed to convey respect through her tiny ever-present smile. But now she erased that pleasantry. Matching the gleam of her pendant, her emerald eyes seemed to pierce mine, to spear straight into my soul — and find uncertainty. I was a marine biologist, damn it, not an expert in conjugal relations. But there was no avoiding the obvious. Something had to be done.

I asked Agata to return to her former chore of cleaning the lab and was gratified she accepted, not with enthusiasm, but without protest.

In grim silence, I fumed at what appeared to be Felicia's blatant infidelity, Ted's infuriating insouciance, and my own inability. Inability? Failure. Failure to do anything about this intolerable situation. The dolt was here by presidential order from my employer. I couldn't fire him, couldn't force him to leave. Was I trapped into just hoping some miracle would change him from philandering fool to helpful employee?

I knew I had to do something. But what?

Our meals became ordeals, with Felicia doing her best to get conversation going, Ted his usual boorish self, and me with anger burning. Ted would push away first. Felicia would linger a bit, but when our strained talk died, she would stride off to the residence.

We lived in a limbo of tension.

***

One sultry evening a month after his arrival, Ted surprised me. After Agata cleared away the dinner dishes, he stayed put. As I watched Felicia walk to the residence, he fiddled with the salt and pepper shakers. Then he said, "What are you trying to prove, Durkin?"

"To prove?"

"You know damn well I'm going to do whatever the hell I want to do around here, but you keep trying. How about a little live and let live?"

"I don't think that's what your uncle expects."

"Yeah. Oliver. This is his idea of 'setting me straight.'" He smirked. "Think it was a good idea?"

"I suspect his purpose was to get you out of circulation up there. What did you do that put you down here?"

"You really want to know?"

"I've wondered."

"It wasn't my fault."

Of course not. The excuse of the chronic failure. I waited.

"First job out of Cornell. Assistant manager at a Hopewell Inn in West Philly. With my creds, I should've been at the Bellevue or at least an Omni. Doing something a couple cuts above handling reservation paperwork."

"When was this?"

"I told you, right out of Cornell when I was twenty-five."

Twenty-five? Had to be a couple of repeated school years in there. "And?"

"And so I told Uncle Oliver what I thought about that lousy assignment. He shipped me off to Europe for a 'change of culture,' as he put it. France, Italy. Supposed to be observing hotel ops over there."

"What had you done at the Hopewell Inn to get you exiled an ocean away?"

He didn't even hesitate. "Nothing. Well, not much of anything. A damned guest from one of those nothing states out west—Dakota, I think—claimed I insulted her."

"Insulted her?"

"Hell, she insulted me. Said I screwed up her and her husband's reservations. Just a little mix-up, that's all. But she wouldn't shut up. We had a...an exchange. And the balloon went up. How was I supposed to know he was a big stockholder and she was mayor of some dumb burg out in cow country? Pair or Pier or something."

"Pierre, maybe?"

"Yeah, that's it."

"You insulted the mayor of the capital of South Dakota?"

"Not my fault."

Good God. "Sure," I said. "How would you know? But exile to the hotels of Europe isn't even close to exile here in the Amazon rain forest. Who'd you kill to deserve this?"

He sighed and slumped back in his chair. "When I got back to the States, Uncle Oliver..."

"Oliver again?"

"It's always Uncle Oliver. My parents were killed in a commuter plane crash when I was in prep school. He took over. Only relative I had left. After the Europe tour, I took a shot at acting — told you about that. When Oliver heard the story, he shipped me to upstate New York. Manager of dining facilities at a four-star ski resort near Rochester. That was where I met Andrea."

Uh oh.

He cradled the back of his head in laced fingers and gazed at the wall behind me. "God, she was pretty. A blond dream in spandex. Innocent as a babe. Took four days to get her out of the damned spandex. What an afternoon that was."

I sat there in the murky twilight listening to the escapades of a thirty-year-old frat boy.

"What a sweet young... Well, that was the problem. How was I to know she was only seventeen? And a virgin, as it turned out. And it also turned out she was the daughter of the president of the holding company that owned the resort. And how was I supposed to know he was a frat brother of Oliver's, a damned Penn State 'Deke'?"

Somebody else's fault again. A failure to communicate. I stared at that face of Errol Flynn in old swashbuckling movies, without the prissy little mustache. Raven hair, deceptively innocent-looking blue eyes. If he'd had any sense, he would have taken the offered bit part and worked up from there. But he didn't have any sense.

"Ted," I asked him, "what do you want to be when you grow up?"

He didn't miss a beat. "I know what I'm going to be when I grow up, Durkin." He shoved back his chair, headed for the door. Turned back. "I'm going to be Uncle Oliver's sole heir."

6

I hunched on the lab stool, elbow on the work shelf, chin propped in my hand. Stared into the compound. I hated Rebner. I hated myself. Did I hate Felicia? She certainly wasn't endearing herself to me.

Heat pressed down in a stifling blanket. I straightened, wiped the sweat off my forehead. Then stared. What in hell were Jheem and Haree up to over there, lugging buckets of water up from the river?

They trudged behind the residence then reappeared, not headed back to their work at the storage shed, but back to the river. Then I realized what they must be doing. Ted, impatient with the currently insufficient roof run-off into our bathing cistern, had them filling it from the river.

My Bororos were working for him. What infuriated me further was his stepping out his front door carrying something folded up, which he opened into our discarded rusted lounge chair. I'd relegated that rickety wreck to the storage shed months ago. As he sprawled on the aged plastic webbing, I hoped it might give way and dump his Royal Arrogance on the wet ground. But no. There in plain view across the compound lounged Uncle Oliver's insolent instigator in sporty blue slacks and pink shirt— pink, for God's sake—no doubt wearing his trademark smirk.

I jumped to my feet, knocking over the stool. I was damned sure going to put a halt to this. I banged the stool back on its legs, stepped toward the screen door…

Then I stopped. River water? Behind me, the bubbling of the aquarium aerators seemed to build into a deafening crescendo. I pulled back. Let Teddy Boy fill the damned cistern. I'd warned him about swimming in the river. I had twice sighted what looked like candirú darting beneath the dock. Not recently, but a catfish not much bigger than a toothpick could easily escape notice.

Let Ted soak to his jaded heart's content. In river water.

A half-hour later, the Bororos trudged back to the west end of the compound and resumed work on the storage building's siding project. A few minutes after that, Ted climbed out of the lounger and headed toward the front entrance of his end of the residence, stripping off his pink shirt as he walked in.

Would he step out the rear door decently attired in bathing trunks? I was willing to give odds he would not. There was nothing decent about the man. He would loll in the cistern naked. The concrete tub was loosely shielded by plywood panels, but I suspected his damned athletic body was by now no mystery to wayward Felicia.

So I waited. Candirús were vicious little devils, quickly burrowing into the urethra with no warning. Once they're in, the opercula spines of each gill cover defy easy extraction. Surgical removal was almost always needed. How appropriate a punishment for philandering Teddy boy. And how convenient for me, I mused. The Polícia Militar maintained a float plane at Santarém for emergency use. Ted would be flown from here probably to the coast for hospitalization and treatment. Out of the Station. Gone.

With the passage of time, I believed I could forgive Felicia. What other reasonable choice would I have if our lives were to return to Station Four's version of normalcy?

I waited. On high alert for the shout of agony that would tell me the inevitable had happened. Waited for the Station's muggy silence to be shattered by a cry of horror behind the residence.

Fifteen minutes... Twenty...

Then Ted stepped from his front doorway in a white shirt this time, rubbing his hair with a towel. Relaxed and refreshed. He sank into the rickety lounger, dropped the towel on the ground and whipped out a pocket comb. A lounger in a lounger, watched by a scientist in a swivet. Depressed by the letdown, I turned away from the front screening to lean back against the work shelf. And my eyes fell on my candirú tank. No candirús in the bathing cistern, but plenty of them right here.

***

Another tense lunch, another virtually silent supper, a cold "good night" to a Felicia whose eyes wouldn't meet mine. I lay in the gray darkness and took refuge in imagination. I could easily scoop a half dozen of the hellish little catfish into a plastic bag, carry it across to the residence under my shirt, and when Ted and Felicia were elsewhere, empty the bag into the cistern. When Ted next dipped into the cistern's waters he apparently regarded as his own--problem solved.

Unfortunately not a foolproof plan. Might Felicia be tempted to join him? Or even bask in the cistern herself before he ventured back in? The timing would have to be exact, or I could very well catch an unintended victim in my trap.

I sighed in frustration. Too uncertain. Too risky to her.

Perhaps... Perhaps there could be a more focused means to purge Station Four of our noxious nephew. The four-foot-long electric eel was out of the question. How could I manage such a cumbersome encounter? The puffer fish? I could easily dissect one of the Gulf puffers, extract the lethal liver, cut it into tiny pieces and manage to slip them into Teddy's scrambled eggs. Then watch him wonder why his lips and tongue were tingling. Why his arms and legs were becoming numb. Why the twitching and tremors? Convulsions next. Then paralysis. There was no treatment for puffer poisoning. No antidote. No need for the emergency seaplane...

My God, I was plotting like a murderer. I would be a murderer. I knew I couldn't do any of these things. I lay there sweating. Obnoxious Ted, no doubt peacefully asleep in the other end of this bare bones building, had just won again. In a struggle he wasn't aware of. And I had lost. Conscience outweighed desperation.

***

Another brittle breakfast. For me, anyway. Ted and Felicia exchanged small talk. I steamed in silence.

Finally, Ted stood, stretched. "I'm going for a walk." And he strode toward the riverbank.

This misery had to stop. Today. Now. I scraped back my chair and followed him.

At the crest of the steep drop-off, he stood hands on hips. The Lord of the Manor surveying his domain? I walked up behind him, and he swung around.

"Yeah?"

"We need to get something straight, Ted. You do not order the Bororos off their assignment to do chores for you. In the future, you will..."

"You don't get it, do you?"

"Get what?"

"Be smart, for once. I'm running this place now. You're the lab man, but I'm actually..."

I felt hot blood rise in my throat. My cheeks burned. "What in hell are you talking about?"

"I'm talking about what's really going on here, Turkey! Turkey Durkin. Has a nice ring to it. Haw, Haw!"

A rush of fury swept through me. Fury at this clod for his incredible insolence, at Felicia for telling him of the nickname that had blighted my teen years. I was hit in the gut by the ancient but enduring frustration Tuffy Tuffare had planted in me. Hot anger dissolved all reason. Fists flailing, I lunged at this hulking idiot.

He laughed. Sidestepped neatly. Slapped the side of my head. I sprawled on hands and knees, my left ear ringing. I glared up at Ted as he spun around to face the compound and threw his arms over his head in a mocking victory salute. "Didja see that, folks?" he shouted to an imaginary audience. Off balance, klutzy Ted stepped back. "Like swatting a fl..." His foot found only air.

I leaped toward him, made a grab for his shirt front. Too late.

He pitched backward down the slope. Bounced. Tumbled, arms and legs flying. With a solid thunk, he slammed into the edge of the dock.

I waited for him to jump to his feet and claw up the bank to finish me off. He didn't move. I scurried down the bank.

"Jesus, Ted. Are you all right?"

His eyes were wide open, unblinking. Then he drew a shuddering breath. Tried to move. Groaned. Slapped a hand on his left hip. And screeched in pain.

"Oh, my God!" Felicia's voice, above us on the crest of the bank.

"Ted fell," I called over my shoulder.

"Is he hurt?"

"I need help here, Felicia. Call the Bororos."

She disappeared. I heard shouting. Then our two Indians plunged down the bank, with Felicia scrambling close behind.

"Accident," I said from my crouch beside Ted's crumpled body.

He groaned. Then he rasped, "Turkey, you bastard. You pu... pushed me..."

"I did no such thing, Ted. I was trying to..."

"I saw it happen, Emmett." Felicia's voice was ice. "How could you?"

"God!" Ted wailed. "It hurts."

I was beyond arguing. "Stay with him. Have the Bororos try to get him up on the dock without more damage." I started up the bank.

"Where are you going?" Felicia demanded.

"To the radio room. To have Picos call the emergency station at Santarém. I think Ted's got a broken hip."

Pushed him! Even in self-inflicted agony, the man was a son of a bitch.

7

No matter how despicable, Ted was a man in major trouble. I burst through the radio room door, gulping for breath. Grabbed the edge of the radio table to keep from falling flat on my face. Scanned the regional map tacked to the wall. Checked its scale. About 150 kilometers of water and jungle between here and Santarém.

I snatched up the one useful thing Sid Warnowski left up here: a small notebook with a mildewed cardboard cover. Mostly blank pages, but he had penciled random notes on the first few, including what I needed — the radio frequency of the distant Santarém emergency station operated by the Policia Militar. Beneath that: "Aircraft, Canadian-built Noorduyn Norseman on floats. Eight-passenger, modified to carry stretchers. Airspeed 150."

When I first tested our radio, I tried to reach Santarém. And failed. The Station's puny transceiver lacked the output to reach that far. I flipped it on and hoped to hell Picos was in his shack — in much closer and in-range — Oriximiná.

"Capitán Picos. Station Four. Do you read me?"

Silence. Sweat ran down my forehead, burned my eyes.

"Picos, are you there? This is Station Four. We have an emergency."

I heard a click.

"Si, Señor Durkin. How can I help?"

Thank God. "We have a man injured here. I need you to contact the Policia Militar's emergency station in Santarém. Pronto."

"Si, Señor Durkin. Rápido."

I gave him their radio frequency. "Tell them we need their seaplane ambulance."

"How much is he hurt?"

"Broken hip, I think."

"Damn! They will have to fly him to Belém. Fine hospital there."

"Muchos gracias, Capitán. As soon as possible."

"Immediato, Señor Durkin."

"Again, thanks. Station Four out."

I shut off the transceiver. Rushed back to the riverbank. Scuttled crabwise down to the dock. Ted's face looked like sweaty bread dough. "I've radioed Picos to contact the police in Santarém," I told him. "They have a rescue-equipped floatplane there. They'll fly you to Belém."

"Belém?" Ted quavered.

"Near the coast. I assume you landed there to begin the boat ride up the Amazon to Oriximiná. It's the Para State capital. I'm told the hospital there has competent surgeons on staff." A bit of an expansion on Picos's calling it a "fine" hospital, but Ted looked as if he could use the encouragement.

"Surgeons," Ted moaned. "Christ! Get me off this damned dock."

"I'm afraid we'd do more damage trying to get you up the bank. I'll bring you a mattress off one of the cots."

"Do that," he snapped.

A few minutes later, I struggled back down lugging a thin mattress and a pillow. I thanked God for holding back the rain. And we waited. With Felicia giving me hard looks between Ted's groans.

"You want some water?" All I got was a scowl. I was sorry to see him leave like this — not at all sorry to see him leave.

Jheem, the taller of our two Bororos, appeared with an umbrella. He'd never go into our residence. Where had it come from? He thrust it into my hand, pointed up the bank.

"Agata," he said.

She was thinking better than I was. I opened the gaily-striped umbrella and placed it to shade Ted's face from the mid-morning sun. I thanked Jheem, motioned him to return to work. He climbed back up the bank.

Felicia and I crouched on the dock's weathered planking.

Waited.

Then she burst out, "Honestly, Emmett. What in God's name was in your head?

"Not now, Felicia. Please."

"Bastard," Ted muttered.

With that, Felicia shook her head, long blond hair flying, and stepped to the foot of the bank.

"Good idea," I told her, "with your sensitivity to the sun. I'll stay here with him 'til the plane comes."

But ten minutes later, she picked her way back down, now carrying a traveling bag. "I'm going with him," she announced.

I was stunned. Was I losing any last hope of resurrecting our marriage? I gaped at her. Words wouldn't come.

"He needs someone with him, Emmett. To help him sign in, check on insurance coverage, arrange for payment... Notify Uncle Oliver."

"I intend to send Oliver a full report, Felicia." Was she doing this for the paperwork? Or was this a cold good-bye — to everything?

"How long will it take them to get here?" Frost in her voice.

"I checked the map in the radio room. Santarém is 150 kilometers from here, straight line." Despite her tone, I welcomed her impersonal question. "That's about ninety-five miles. According to Warnowski's moldy notebook, the plane could make 150 miles an hour. So, assuming Picos had managed an immediate relay of what I told him. And they didn't get held up on take-off clearances, I'd guess they would be here in an hour or so. Maybe less."

We hunkered uncomfortably on the dock's hard boards. Heavy planking over a substructure of tightly lashed empty oil drums. Held to shore by two heavy nylon lines. Each line was secured to a metal stake driven halfway up the bank. One line angled upstream, the other downstream. The river current held the dock to the foot of the bank, the upstream line pivoting on its stake as the water level rose or fell.

Beneath the blanket, Ted shuddered, probably edging toward shock. Felicia hunched with her arms around her upraised knees, staring across the placid river. Silent as the sluggishly flowing water.

I sat cross-legged, arms propped behind me, trying to sort out my tangled reactions. Elated over Ted's imminent departure, but depressed he had been seriously injured. Relieved help was on the way, but stunned that Felicia was leaving with him. Gratified Ted's injury was self-inflicted, but anguished over Felicia's ready acceptance of his accusation that I pushed him. An awful hour for all three of us crept along in bitter silence.

***

Then I heard the approaching drone of the rescue plane. It flashed into view around the river's south bend, banked left and roared toward us. Its big radial engine vibrated the dock planking as it raced overhead, a bright red, high-winged monoplane with a pair of huge pontoons.

Engine howling through a long swing southward, the plane reappeared over the distant shore. Sunlight flashed on the broad scarlet wing as the pilot lined up to land into the light westerly breeze. The engine's bellow faded. The plane dropped below the distant shore's tree line. Its twin floats split the water in a creamy wake. It settled then taxied toward the dock. The pilot gunned it briefly to swerve sideways and cut power. As the big right side pontoon bumped the dock's front edge, the co-pilot, a stubby man in rumpled khakis, jumped down on the starboard pontoon with a line to moor the float to a dock cleat.

The pilot stepped from cabin to pontoon to dock, a wiry, copper-skinned man. His trim mustache, visored cap, and leather jacket seemed to amplify a flyer's vanity.

"Boa tarde, senhor," he said to me then nodded at Ted. "Our passenger?"

"They both are your passengers. My wife is going with Senhor Rebner."

"She is uma enfermeira...a nurse?"

"No." I tried to keep my voice steady. "She is going with him to... help."

The pilot nodded at Ted again. "The senhor's ferimento?"

"What?" I asked Felicia, her Portuguese far better than mine.

"His injury, I think."

"Oh. Broken. Here." I patted my left hip. "He'll need help getting aboard."

The pilot said something to the co-pilot, who nodded, hopped back on the pontoon, reached into the plane, slid open a large hatchway behind the pilots' access and hauled out two poles rolled in canvas. They unfurled the stretcher and eased it beneath Ted with impressive gentleness, I thought. Then all four of us managed to lift the stretcher over the pontoon and through the opening behind the cockpit access door, modified, I assumed, to accommodate stretcher-borne passengers. With the pilot's assistance, Felicia climbed from the pontoon into the passenger section, carefully stepping over Ted to sit in one of the four seats along the far side. She hadn't said a word of good-bye.

The co-pilot unhitched the mooring line, rolled it up, tossed it aboard. Both pilots climbed in. The doors slammed shut. The pilot shouted something and I stepped back. The big propeller flipped over, caught and shimmered. With a roar and a belch of blue smoke, the Noorduyn eased away from the dock, taxied fast across the river, made a wide 180 near the far shore to face into the wind. The engine thundered. The plane headed straight for me, grew huge, lifted and blasted over the Station to fade in the steamy afternoon.

I plodded back up the steep bank. When I reached the crest, I stood there staring at the drab buildings, silent beneath the treetops arching over the clearing. There went two people who had betrayed me. The Bororos and Agata remained, but they had isolated me behind their wall of disdain. I was alone.

I had no appetite but walked to the mess hut for a cup of coffee. Agata, in her shapeless tan smock, gave me a look that was...what? Accusatory? Or only puzzled? Whatever she was thinking, it prompted me to take my coffee to the lab, where I immersed myself in my notes on the electric eel. A snake, Ted called it. Snake, for God's sake. Four hundred discharges per second, up to 600 volts each. Some "snake."

Agata arrived to clean but now carried a tray with a fresh pot of coffee, sugar and powdered creamer.

"Obrigada, Agata," I said with some surprise. "I appreciate this."

She nodded, seized a broom and began to work her way along the aquarium rows. Then she stopped. "Senhor Rebner is gone?" she asked in her accented English.

"Yes. And so is Senhora Durkin."

She gave me a long, indecipherable look. Then she said, "I am sorry about Senhora Durkin."

"Thank you."

"But," she added, as she resumed her sweeping, "not about Senhor Rebner."

***

I lay on my cot. Peered up into darkness. In the aftermath of a rainsquall, an insect chorus chirred and rasped around the residence. Even in here, the air held its peaty tang of dank vegetation.

I still burned over Ted's lying accusation. Pushed, he'd said. That one word, and Felicia turned to ice. Even claimed she'd seen me do it! How could she possibly believe that?

Ted's presence had destroyed Station Four's discipline then corrupted its morality. Good damned riddance. His plunge down the bank was not my doing. Well, maybe indirectly. No, damn it! His own nutty posturing after my pathetic lunge put him down the bank.

And had apparently cost me my wife.

8

I n the north end of the storage building, I bent over the radio table. Flipped on the transceiver already tuned to the frequency of the radio in Capitán Picos's "fleet headquarters," his riverside shack in Oriximiná. He lived in that two-room shanty, conducted business there and moored his steam launch to the adjacent warped-board dock. Ostentation was not his strong point; dependability was.

I keyed the mike. "Station Four, Capitán Picos. Do you read?"

"Si, Señor Durkin. Go 'head," urged the metallic voice of Ramon Picos. The little Mexican expatriate had finessed the contract to serve as Station Four's contact with the outside world by radio as well as by boat. I was reminded again this tough little Mexican expatriate served as our lifeline to civilization.

"I need you to send a telegram."

"Si, telegrama."

"A telegram to Oliver Rebner at the Foundation in Philadelphia. You have the address."

"Si. Señor Rebner in Philadelphia."

"You have a pencil? Take this down carefully, Capitán. ACCIDENT HAS..."

"Accidente! Qué ha pasado?"

"Just take this down, Captain" ACCIDENT HAS PUT TED—that's T-E-D—in BELÉM HOSPITAL. SUSPECT BROKEN HIP. WILL MAIL DETAILED REPORT."

I hesitated.

"Si, Señor Durkin. That is it?"

Hell, I decided to bite the bullet. "Add this: RECOMMEND TED BE RECALLED TO RECUPERATE. That is it, Captain. Read it back, please."

Despite his accent and seeming casualness, Picos repeated my message with a question about the spelling.

"Two Ms in RECOMMEND and R-E-C-U in RECUPERATE," I told him. That settled, I added, "Good work, amigo. See that it is sent off promptly. Add the cost to the Station's monthly account. Gracias and buenos dias, Capitân. Station Four out."

That, I hoped, would wrap up the flagrant south-of-the-border career of Theodore Rebner. As for Felicia, I suspected our marriage had taken the fall even before Ted took his. I had little doubt an alarmed Uncle Oliver would immediately ring up Felicia's family, and they would insist on her return. If — as I was beginning to wonder — Oliver Rebner's intent on sending the two of us here was to strain our marriage to the breaking point. If so, it had worked — but only after Ted swaggered upon the scene.

As I shut down the radio, a truly boggling thought struck me. Could Oliver, with the Noonans' complicity, actually have sent his womanizing nephew here as a disruptive agitator? No, no. Such speculation would get me nowhere.

Whatever had impelled Felicia's blatant behavior, here I sat struggling with depression. Without even the comfort of Sid Warnowski's pinch bottle.

Three station chiefs in not quite four years. The first, Picos had confided, had been steam-launched out of here wracked with the moaning meemies. I had witnessed the second, Warnowski, boated away in alcoholic miasma. Station chief number three, one disillusioned Emmett Durkin, remained on post. Bereft of unfaithful wife — and the unprincipled bastard who engineered her fall from secluded grace.

What would Felicia do now? I wondered. Ted's attraction had to be without real substance. She was an intelligent woman. The appeal of such an oaf had to be no more than a hormonal rush. He was a good-looking guy; I'd give him that. Well-built with that damned Errol Flynn face — and Flynn's libido, come to think of it. But damned if I could believe she walked out on me for that...that bastard!

To hell with all this speculation. It was going nowhere. Back to work, Emmett. In the lab.

Through an apprehensive week, I struggled with the written report I knew the Foundation would insist on my filing. And I waited — dreaded — Oliver's response to my hasty telegram. I attempted productive lab work, was crisply civil to Agata and the two Bororos, though I wondered what was going through their jungle-wise brains. On the seventh day of emptiness, the little red bulb in the lab flashed on. Picos calling.

In a sweat, I jogged the length of the compound, tore open the storage building's north-end door. Plunked down on the stool in front of the transceiver — then hesitated. Did I really want to hear this? Hear the words that would confirm what I already suspected but didn't want confirmed? Hear that Felicia had fled back to Philadelphia, and I faced a bleak, hopeless...

I flipped the transceiver switch. "Station Four."

"Señor Durkin? Capitán Picos aqui. I have a wire."

My mouth dried. My voice cracked. "Re...read it, please." Be optimistic. With luck, I might even be called to Philadelphia to work on the civilized end of all this jungle research.

Picos cleared his throat. I heard paper rustle. "It say only: 'CARRY ON.'"

"What?"

"That is all it say. 'CARRY ON.'"

What in hell did that mean? Apparently only that I was still on the Foundation payroll. Oliver Rebner was so distressed he could trust himself to wire only two words?

Carry on?

My stomach leaped into my throat. My heart thudded louder in my ears than the generator's throb. Sweat drenched my polo shirt. Carry on alone in this soggy oven of an outpost?

Then I had the queasy feeling more was going on behind that terse message. But what? With just two words, Oliver Rebner had consigned me to limbo.

***

On my walk back to the lab, I paused. The thrum of the generator had deepened.

No, that wasn't the generator. I was hearing a boat engine — and not Picos's decrepit barge. Picos had just radioed me from Oriximiná.

I trotted through the cloying humidity to the crest of the riverbank. A cabin cruiser — a forty-footer, I judged — nosed into view around the river's south bend. Its bow wave diminished as the helmsman reduced power. Some millionaire playboy passing through on a ramble up the Amazon's tributaries?

Then my heart stuttered. At her stern, she flew the green flag of Brazil with its blue orb in a yellow diamond.

The boat veered toward the dock. I made out four men, including the helmsman on the enclosed forward section. He shifted the propeller into reverse. The cruiser nudged the dock. One of the three in the open cockpit aft leaped out to secure bow and stern lines to the dock cleats. All wore khaki uniforms.

The ranking officer, I assumed by way of his extra brassware, stepped up on the gunwale then down on the dock. The man who secured the lines hopped back aboard. The one who debarked took off his cap, a police officer's visored cap. He wiped his forehead with a blue bandanna, stuffed it back in his hip pocket, slapped the cap back on then gazed up at me.

I barely nodded. I felt no compulsion to go down there to greet this unsettling visitor. Arms folded, I stood my ground and watched the squat officer with his drooping mustache make his way up the bank. He was muscular, but his thick middle suggested a lot of time in his office.

"Capitão Rolha," the officer said as he panted over the crest. "Pará Polícia Militar. Based in Santarém"

"Capitão." I shook Rolha's outstretched hand. The man's powerful grip was as sweaty as mine. "What can I do for you?"

"You are in charge here? You are Senhor Durkin?" His English was heavily accented but apparently fluent. Any thought I had of deflecting an investigator with a language barrier was not going to work with Rolha.

I nodded. "Can I offer you coffee?"

"Obrigado, Senhor Durkin. Obrigado."

In the mess hut, the capitão tossed his cap on the table and wiped his brow again. "A hot day."

"Always, in this part of Brazil." My casualness was forced. Surely, this state cop had more on his mind than the weather.

Rolha had the narrow eyes and, beneath the mustache, the unsmiling mouth of a born investigator. His wiry black hair capped his avocado-shaped head in tight ripples. His eyes focused on Agata as she carried in the coffee tray. Since we had come in here, I noticed, Rolha couldn't seem to keep his eyes off her. Yet the police officer's gaze didn't appear to be one of lust.

Rolha held up his coffee mug. "À sua saúde, Senhor Durkin!" A toast? The cop took a long pull at his coffee then leaned back in his chair.

"Now we attend to business. Of concern is the event involving..." He pulled a little black notebook from his shirt pocket. Flipped a few pages. "Ah, sim. Here it is. The event involving Senhor Rebner, Theodore. I have spoken with the pilot of our emergency airplane, and with hospital authorities in Belém. Now I speak with you."

"An unfortunate accident." I tried to hit the proper note of dismay. "Do you know how he is?"

"You have not heard?"

"We are very isolated here."

"Senhor Rebner's left hip was badly broken. It has been repaired."

"I'm glad to hear that."

Rolha held up a forefinger. "Repaired, sim. But the surgeon expects a condition."

"Condition?"

"Sim. A fine surgeon who did his best work, but he tells me Senhor Rebner will have a limp."

"A limp. For how long?"

"Who knows? The damage was great. But he can walk. That is the important thing, is it not?"

"Of course," I said. Poetic justice after all? High stepping Ted was not now stepping so high.

"I regret to tell you Senhor Rebner has made certain accusations," Rolha went on with no change in his stony expression. "That, in fact, is why I make this visit."

My throat went dry. I reached for my coffee. The mug was empty. "Agata!" Almost a croak. "More coffee, por favor." I turned back to Rolha. His eyes were on Agata again. Narrowing to slits.

"Most people after a fall like his," I said, "into the edge of a dock, would be happy to walk at all."

"Sim, senhor." His eyes lingered on Agata. Then he turned to me. "But that is not the point. Senhor Rebner claims he had, uh, some assistance…"

"We did immediately call for help, Capitão. And made him as comfortable as possible."

"Of course. But that was at the bottom of his fall. He claims assistance at the top." The coal-black, slitty eyes held mine.

Ted, you lying son of a bitch.

"Senhor?" Rolha prompted.

"I'll tell you exactly what happened, Capitão. The man had become useless. Arrogant. Defiant. That morning at the riverbank, I tried to talk some sense into him. I'll admit I was angry. In fact, I lost my temper. Rushed at him."

"You rushed at him?"

"Yes. But he just shoved me aside, knocked me off my feet. And laughed. Then, as I was getting back up, he went into a stupid sort of victory dance. Stepped backward. Lost his balance. I tried to grab him, but too late. He fell down the bank. Accidentally."

I picked up my coffee mug, willing my fingers not to tremble. Took a swallow. Set the mug down. "That, Capitão, is the absolute truth."

He looked at me. I met his gaze, trying desperately to stay impassive. Cool. Cool, in this tropical heat?

Finally, he gazed down at his mug. Slowly twirled it. Then the shrewd unblinking eyes flicked back up at me. "Senhor, I believe you are an honest man. About Senhor Rebner, I had not a good feeling. Your wife I also spoke with. She said she saw Senhor Rebner fall."

I held my breath.

"But she said she was too far away to be sure of what happened."

I breathed again. That was not at all what I expected.

"And now that we have met, senhor, I make an observation. Senhor Rebner is a large man with much muscle — and much arrogance. You are… not so large." He paused, peered at the ceiling, then at his hands. Then at me. "So unless some proof to the contrary arises," he said slowly, "I must consider the unfortunate happening an accident."

With relief, I scraped back my chair. "I appreciate your thoroughness, Capitão. I don't want to hold you up. I know it's a long trip back to Santarém."

He held up his hand, palm out. "There may be another matter." He turned to Agata, standing in silence at the far end of the kitchen area. "Como se chama?"

"Agata," she said. "Agata Lagoa."

"Interessante." Now Rolha wore a tight little smile. "A woman, also a cook, is wanted in Manaus. Pérola Portel. She is accused of a serious crime during the rainy season last year."

I shot a quick glance at Agata, motionless near the doorway to her bedroom. Lose her, and despite the presence of the Bororos, I would feel truly alone. Her healthy bronze complexion seemed to have paled. My imagination? Her eyes met mine, but they conveyed nothing.

"She came here before the past rainy season," I lied. "That would be just about a year ago."

Rolha's heavy eyebrows rose. He leaned toward me, dropping his voice to a near-whisper. "Your cook…"

"She is our housekeeper…and cook."

"She appears to match the description of the Portel woman. Tall for an Indian crossbreed, with the same light brown eyes — and bonita, muita bonita."

"Even I am aware, Capitão, this is a country of many races and intermingling is encouraged by your government."

Agata stood impassive, meeting Rolha's stare, not hearing our muted words, I hoped.

The police official glanced at his big wristwatch. "I have another stop to make. Upriver, unfortunately." He took another long look at Agata.

Then he shrugged. "The Portel woman did not flee Manaus until after the last rainy season. And, as you say, your woman arrived before the rainy season began."

I almost told him she came to us not from Manaus, but from the Hotel Uirapura in Santarém. Held that back just in time. Too easy for him to check out and discover I was lying about the time of her arrival. She had heard from a friend of Capitán Picos about the Station's need for a housekeeper and arrived here in his grubby launch just five months ago.

"What is the Portel woman wanted for?" I asked.

"Eh? Ah, assault, senhor. She stabbed her marido — her husband. With a fish knife. He survived but has lost the full use of his arm." He spoke to me but kept his eyes on Agata. Raising his voice, he asked, "You have papers, Agata Lagoa?"

She never wavered. "Lost, Capitáo. The trip here in a small boat. There was a surprise storm."

Rolha's icy fixation on her seemed to last forever. Then he sighed, rammed back his chair. Stood. "It is the life of the polícia to be always suspicious. I must begin the trip back before the day is older. Obrigado, senhor, for your hospitality."

We walked together toward the riverbank. I was tense with fear that any moment, Rolha would turn back to question Agata more thoroughly.

But when I stopped at the bank's crest, Rolha gave me a quick salute and murmured, "Boa sorte, senhor. Good luck." With that, the state police officer made his way down the bank to his boat.

The powerful engine kicked in. One of the deckhands cast off and leaped back aboard. The big cruiser rumbled away in a wide upriver swing. The bow rose, carving a long V of foamy wake and the boat thrummed out of view to the north. As the engine noise faded, rain began to dimple the water then filter through the compound's canopy.

I walked back to the lab unable to shake my gnawing concern that Rolha's benign departure might not mark the end of the Ted Rebner incident, but only the end of the beginning.

9

An evening downpour drummed the metal roof of the residence. I slumped at the makeshift desk, two ten-inch boards on a pair of battered green two-drawer filing cabinets. Their rusted scratches and dents told me they probably had been here since the Station was established. When Felicia and I arrived a year ago, I slid open the four squealing file drawers to find only a scatter of incomprehensible notes, apparently Warnowski's, with Haig & Haig as co-authors. Now copies of my reports to the Foundation lay in the top drawer of the cabinet on the right. Perhaps useful for a future book. Perhaps useless to this prospective book author, already struggling with writer's block over the report I promised Oliver.

Carry on?

Had he simply run out of words to convey his alarm at the whole miserable situation here? Or could his reaction be a British-like stiff-upper-lip order to a station chief in a bind? Carry on as if Ted had never tumbled down the bank? As if Felicia hadn't deserted me?

I felt a sardonic twinge. Carrion, perhaps? Had Picos made a phonetic adjustment to a telephoned telegram? Was the message a fit-of-temper epithet from a thoroughly disgusted Oliver? Pack up, Durkin, you're dead meat?

No, no. Picos had reported "it say," indicating he was reading a delivered telegram, not "they say," were he reporting a phone call from the Oriximiná telegraph office.

I sat back and shook my head. Jesus, I didn't need Warnowski's bottle. I was becoming addled all on my own. The report, Durkin. The report. From the left cabinet, I assembled two sheets of paper with carbon paper between. No Xerox machines in this neck of the forest. Picked up a pen and forced myself to get at it.

I scrawled the date and began, "At approximately 9 a.m., 10 October, I approached Theodore Rebner, who was standing on the crest of the Station's riverbank..." I plodded on with the same accurate details I had given Pará Polícia Militar Capitáo Rolha. But I added a fairly dramatic account of the aerial rescue operation. Again, I recommended Ted Rebner's recall to benefit his health, I wrote — not to mention my own. And, I did not add, anybody else's here — though only Agata, the day-shift Bororos and I remained. Felicia's departure, I covered gracefully, I hoped. "In an act of kindness, my wife accompanied Ted to Belém to assist him with the inevitable paperwork complications of hospital admittance and payment. She intends to meet expenses via the Foundation's VISA or Mastercard accounts, which I assume will be acceptable procedure."

I finished my "creative non-fiction" piece with an assurance I would indeed "carry on" and assured Oliver the Station's work would be unaffected by the unfortunate episode.

Signed the thing, folded it, slid it into an envelope. Picos would take it on his next trip up here and mail it in Oriximiná.

As I sat back, satisfied with my effort, the rain increased to an overhead roar. Just as the generator reached its scheduled cut-off time, I crawled onto my creaky cot. And pondered. Until the damned "carry on" telegram, I'd occasionally had a wildly optimistic hope: Oliver could be thinking of pulling me out of here for work in his Philadelphia headquarters. A stupid, totally unfounded daydream. Now, I found it more likely Oliver's cryptic message could be a tactic to keep me in place while he came up with something more drastic for the villain who had "pushed" his only heir down the bank.

Would I give a damn if he did? Yes, I would. Because completing a full two-year assignment in this remote post would look damned good in my curriculum vitae. For that same reason, I was painfully aware, I could not just quit, hop on Picos's steam launch, and get the hell out of here.

***

Through the next few days, the shock of Capitão Rolha's visit diminished. Agata's Mona Lisa smile returned. She went about her tasks humming an unrecognizable melody, some obscure folk tune, I assumed. What impressed me more was the morning she had literally let her hair down. Freed from its confining braid, an ebony wave fell below her shoulders in a lustrous shimmer. At breakfast, I caught myself staring.... The isolation. You'll find out.

I broke my stare. But not before I caught her tiny smile widening a fraction.

Except for my inability to forget Rolha's visit, I was relieved Station Four was easing back into its pre-Rebner peacefulness. Though I still smarted over Felicia's emotional blast concerning Ted's tumble down the bank, I truly missed her reassuring companionship before Ted had corrupted her. So I found this to be hollow tranquility, better in only one way. Better without Ted haunting every waking moment.

Then the totally unexpected happened. At supper, I finished the sweet fruit dessert Agata had prepared — goiabada, she called it. As she cleared away my dish and turned toward the kitchen area, I felt a gentle pressure on my shoulder. Her hand lingered only a moment. But such an intimate touch from an employee triggered in me a reflex of resentment at such familiarity. My housekeeper-cook actually…well, caressed her employer.

Then I felt an undeniable rush of warmth. And embarrassment. I had no idea how to react. Her fingers trailed away. I heard her set the dish on the drain board. After a long pause of uncertainty, I forced myself to rise then stand awkwardly at the kitchen entrance. She had her back to me. What should I say? Should I say anything?

"Thank…" I cleared my suddenly dry throat. "Thank you, Agata. That was a fine meal."

She turned from the sink, head tilted down, warm brown eyes peering up into mine. Her smile deepened.

"Obrigado, Senhor Durkin. It is I who thanks you."

"You thank me?"

With her hair flowing free, she seemed ten years younger. An unexpectedly lovely woman.

"Sim. For what you told Capitão Rolha. I owe you much."

"You owe me nothing, Agata."

"Senhor Durkin, what you did means my life. I owe you a great debt."

I was impressed with her earnestness. With a twinge of shame, I realized I had never considered her more than competent menial help. Now, her simple, tender gesture had jolted me into seeing her from an unsettling new perspective, but I was uncertain about its import.

"You don't owe me a thing, Agata." I turned away before I could embarrass myself with some even more clumsy response. "Good night."

"Boa noite, Senhor Durkin."

I strode into twilight still golden with sunset's afterglow.

"She's hired help, Emmett, and that's how you will behave toward her. Civil but not familiar." My mother's voice, recalled, as I stepped into the warm darkness of the residence. She preached an uncrossable line between domestic and employer. For a year or so, she had been stricken with some elusive illness that impelled my father to hire a cook-helper five days a week. Maggie Walsh's weekly stipend was a drain on Dad's high-school English teacher's earnings, but Maggie's eager helpfulness was more of a drain on my mother's rigid sense of class. She was forever rousting me, ten or twelve years old at the time, from hilarious kitchen conversations with "the help," as Mother never failed to term Maggie. "She is hired help, Emmett, and that's how you will behave toward her. Civil but not familiar."

Young as I was, I thought that was a stuffy, outdated attitude. Now I found it had stuck with me. Wasn't that precisely how I had been treating Agata? Civil but not familiar? She was, after all, just hired help.

By breakfast time next morning, I had become fully aware how ridiculous that attitude was, here in the Brazilian rainforest, far from anything remotely resembling the social structures of civilization as I had lived it.

As I entered the mess shack, I said—hastily, before I could change my mind—"Agata, I would like you to join me for breakfast." With that, I broached the barrier my mother had instilled in me more than a decade ago.

With plate, mug and a near-radiant smile, Agata stepped into the dining area. For the first time since she had arrived, she had forsaken her drab Mother Hubbard smock. As if she had somehow predicted my invitation, now she wore a long, gaily-colored sleeveless dress that fully revealed her flawless throat. From a drab cocoon, a lovely butterfly had emerged.

Despite my effort to move a bit beyond "civil," I felt awkward with this increasingly attractive woman no longer hovering subserviently about the dining area, but now sitting across from me at the table. The silence became uncomfortable.

"Tell me, if you wish to," I blurted, "about Manaus."

Agata put down her fork and folded her arms over her breasts, as if she were shielding herself from the act of telling. For a long moment, she sat silent. The only sound was the ping of morning dew dropping from the tree canopy onto the hut's tin roof. Have I gone too far, I wondered, in this uneasy new relationship?

Then, eyes on her plate, she said, "He was a cruel man, Senhor Durkin. Muito mau. I gave him everything I could. But he beat me. Many times."

Then her cocoa eyes met mine. "I said nada. But when he went with another woman, I told him adeus. In the kitchen, he hit hard. I took a fish knife. He hit me more." She looked down again. "And I...I gave him the blade."

I stared at her.

"He fell on the floor with much blood. Then I ran. I thought I killed him. But I heard Capitão Rolha say he lives. I don't know if I am happy with that or unhappy."

When I started breathing again, I said, "It seems to me a competent lawyer could make a case for justifiable self-defense. Why did you run?"

"Because my husband works for the polícia."

"He is a police officer?"

"No, a clerk, but still polícia. I hid. Then got on a boat to Santarém."

"Where…" I cleared my throat, tried again…"where you found work at the Hotel Uirapura."

"Sim. As a housekeeper. But in Manaus, as I truly told you when I came here, I was assistant chef at Hotel Mônaco.

The most compelling aspect of her confession was her lack of bitterness. If bitterness was ever justified, her experience deserved a share. Yet I heard none. Remarkable.

She raised her coffee mug with slender fingers that trembled, just slightly. Gave me a quick glance, then her eyes again dropped to the table's rough boards.

"Why did you leave Santarém, Agata? Why did you come here?" Delving into her personal life made me feel uneasy, but it kept the conversation going.

"A friend told me the police still looked. She knew Capitão Picos made trips to places where the polícia do not often go. One place was here, and Capitão Picos told me of the need for a cook."

Made sense. Our need for a cook. Her need for obscurity. And now I knew why she had arrived with three suitcases. All she owned. She had nowhere else to go.

Another silence.

I took a hefty swallow of now-cold coffee. Set down the mug with an unintended clunk. "Your English, Agata. Where did you learn it?"

Her smile returned, teeth startlingly white against her russet lips and bronze skin. "My father. He was Irish. Miner of emeralds in Colombia before he went to Manaus to work on buildings." She fingered her ever-present pendant. "This is what I have from him. It is Colombian, darker than Brazil emeralds."

"It's a beautiful stone," I said. "And your mother?"

"My mother, mestiza. Indian and Portuguese. A cook at Caçarola."

"Caçarola?"

"A restaurante in Manaus. From her, I learn to cook."

"And they?"

"'They'?"

"Your parents. Are they still in Manaus?"

"Não, senhor. After I am married, my mother, she died. My father, when he lost his job in Manaus, he had to leave me. To go back to the Colombia mines."

"I'm sorry," I said. And wondered what to say next.

Into the awkward silence, I blurted, "Do you like it here?"

Her eyes rose and caught mine. Her voice was no more than a murmur. "It is…muito lonely."

"Yes. It is."

We sat silent in the silent morning. Confessed husband stabber and forsaken scientist. Nothing in common but loneliness. A prospect to be endured over the remaining year of my contractual obligation.

"Agata," I said. "I would like you to join me for every meal."

Her face brightened. "Sim, senor. I would like that muito.... Very much."

10

Not acceptable behavior. Not at all. I shouldn't have invited Agata to share my table. Mother would be appalled. But I believed maintaining a master-servant relationship between us two remaining station residents would be ridiculously pompous.

Circumstances had made Agata and me entirely dependent on each other. My only other social contact, if I could call it that, was Indy's occasional reappearance—almost as if the big, blue-black snake sensed my loneliness. Ridiculous, of course, but I took pleasure in his long, silent stares before he slithered gracefully back into the forest's understory behind the residence.

Agata had been a nearly invisible servant. Now I was discovering she was intelligent beyond her station. With her baggy smock—muumuu as I called it—replaced by colorful frocks, Agata emerged as a vibrantly attractive woman. Slender, well-shaped legs, slim waist, perky bosom... Stop it, Durkin. You're staring.

Emmett Durkin, I reproached myself, you are an idiot. Stop this before it spins out of hand. But why? For a traitorous wife who by now was surely gone? For an employer who had consigned me to lonely exile?

Our mealtime closeness continued.

One murky afternoon, Capitán Picos chuffed in with his scheduled mid-month delivery of staples. As the barrel-shaped boatman and I sat together in the mess shack for our now-traditional coffee respite, his thick eyebrows shot upward. His gaze was riveted on Agata in her gay flowered dress, her lustrous ebony mane eye-riveting. She gave Picos a smiling nod.

"Dios, Señor Durkin!" he breathed, leaning toward me. "Muy hermosa."

"Hermosa?" My Spanish was no better than my Portuguese.

"Good looking," Picos whispered, his eyes still on her. "More than that."

"True, Capitán...Capitán?"

Reluctantly, he turned back to me with a sly grin. "Si?"

I handed him the addressed envelope with my detailed report to Oliver. "For mailing, as soon as you return to Oriximiná."

"Ah, si." He glanced at his watch. "Time to go." He stood, bowed to Agata.

"A Dios, señorita." Nodded at me. "Señor." Clapped on his stained yachting cap and strode back to the riverbank.

***

She walked into the lab the next morning in another of her charming flower-print dresses. I felt the same sense of warmth I'd experienced at breakfast. The midmorning coffee she brought had become another excuse to have her near me.

She put down the tray with a cheery, "Bom dia — again, senhor."

"Agata, you needn't call me 'senhor' as if I'm a visiting stranger."

She smiled, a touch impishly, I thought. "What then, senhor, should I call you?"

I'd set my own trap. "Amigo, perhaps?"

"Friend? Herói would be better."

"Not if it means what it sounds like. 'Amigo' will do."

"Sim...amigo." She glanced at the work shelf. "Why all this?" Her voice was close to my ear. Warm. Musical.

Why all this? A question Felicia had never asked, but one I had begun to ask myself.

"For science, Agata. I send information and biological materials to Philadelphia. "They..." Exactly what do they do with it? I wondered, not for the first time.

"Sim,...amigo?"

"They use the information to, uh, increase their knowledge of these dangerous species," I told her. Lamely, I felt.

Her eyes still held her question, but she nodded and began to sweep the walkways between the tank rows.

What in hell did they do up there in the City of Brotherly Love with all my details on the care and feeding of marine menaces? "Scientific research," Oliver had said. I was aware of Bill Haast's work at his Florida Serpentarium, first in Miami then in Tampa. He extracted snake venom, shipped it to a pharmaceutical firm in Baltimore. There the venom was processed into antivenin. I assumed the Foundation was doing essentially the same thing — at least with the puffer fish, stingray and frog toxins.

I stared into the empty compound. A brilliant blue and yellow macaw dived beneath the trees' canopy and glided toward the river.

What about the rest of my scary aquaria? Perhaps military applications? A swarm of candirús released in a stream where enemy soldiers bathed? A couple of electric eels to add to the mayhem? A school of defensive stingrays established at potential landing beaches? Probably not effective against booted landing parties...

My speculations seemed a tad far-fetched, more like grist for horror fiction mills than practical military applications. But if the Foundation was willing to underwrite all this, who was I to question its practicality?

***

Between rainsqualls that afternoon, I wandered to the riverbank. Gazed down at the floating dock. Minimal but practical. The only quality equipment here was the Boston Whaler—which, I reminded myself, needed a battery-boosting jaunt across the river and back. Aside from the Whaler, everything here at the Station would delight a skinflint of a corporate finance officer. Frame and tin buildings. Cots, not beds. Camp furniture. Generator and radio adequate, but not what I would consider even close to top-of-the-line.

Were the other three Stations put together like this one? Built on the cheap? They certainly were as geographically remote as Station Four. One along the Chani River in Chad. Cobras and crocodiles, I supposed. Another Station on Ulang Island in the Palaus. Sea snakes and jellyfish? The third, according to the Foundation's Annual Report, worked in the Australian Outback. A wealth of dangerous fauna there.

All four Stations were located where visitation would be difficult and unlikely. All of us submitting findings that surely sounded of value. But in our hearts did we all wonder, as I found myself wondering now: to what real purpose?

Four remote facilities. Highly touted in Foundation publicity output. Impressive for any contribution-supported foundation, and for this one which existed entirely on grants and donated funds.

Returning to the lab, I stared at my notebook, struggling against my suspicion Station Four—and the other three—were at best providing limited scientific information on dangerous biota. To what end, I had no specific knowledge. At worst, though, stripped of Annual Report PR, were we all set up on the cheap as scientific window dressing to attract donations, organizational grants, and perhaps grants from less-than-meticulous government agencies with taxpayer money to give away? When one can secure a federal grant to study the methane in cow farts, where was the limit?

Had Warnowski—and Melvin Proctor before him—gone through to this same speculation, a conjecture that crippled then destroyed them?

***

I needed a break. Oh, how I needed a break. "Agata," I said after breakfast the following day, "the rain has let up and the boat can use a run to keep up its battery." I was tempted to add, the same applied to me. But I said, "Would you like to come along?"

She looked up from her plate with a bright smile. "Oh, sim, amigo. I would like very much. But I must clean the dishes..."

"Hell with the dishes. Let's go."

"Um minuto, por favor." She rushed through the kitchen area into her room beyond, emerging a couple minutes later with a yellow scarf tied under her chin, a bright accent to her red and yellow dress.

I had the boat key in my pocket. We walked to the crest of the bank and I took her arm to help her down. With the rainy season in its early weeks, the river had risen, but only a few inches. Together we rolled back the canvas boat cover, folded it on the dock. I stepped aboard. Slipped the key into the ignition. Let down the upraised ninety-horse Johnson outboard until its propeller was underwater. Put the gears in neutral and cranked up the engine. After a couple of smoky blaps, it idled smoothly. Taking her arm, I steadied Agata as she stepped aboard. I seated her on the captain's bench behind the midship console. I untied the fore and aft mooring lines from their dock cleats, stowed them aboard, joined her on the bench seat and eased the throttle forward. The engine purred sweetly as we glided away from the dock into the broad Trombetas.

The current flowed just a few knots stronger than its normal slow drift. Heeding my own directive, I swung upstream. A hundred yards offshore, we paralleled the west bank for a few miles. Then emboldened by the serenity of the sun-speckled river, I turned east to head straight across. I eased the throttle forward. The Johnson began to howl. The bow rose. I got her "up on the step." We leveled off and raced toward the distant tree line.

I glanced at Agata. Her eyes danced. Her smile widened to a delighted grin, teeth flashing. "Oh, amigo!" she shouted over the engine's bellow, "This is so...so excitante!" She yanked off the headscarf, shook her hair free. God, I thought, she is absolutely radiant.

Fifty yards off the east shore, I eased back the throttle, swung us south to parallel the towering jungle over here. A flock of green and yellow Amazon parrots burst from a stand of kapok trees, squawked in protest at our intrusion, then wheeled inland. Across the river, I could just make out the Station's stretch of riverbank scarring the shoreline. I swung us west and we began a leisurely return.

"Obrigada, amigo," Agata beamed as I eased the Whaler back to the dock. "That was maravilhosa." Hand cradling her elbow, I steadied her as she stepped back to the dock. I re-secured the mooring lines and we stretched the cover back in place. Then we climbed up the slope to the compound.

"And now," she said in a tone I found...well, teasing, "I am going to do something I must do."

"What can that be?" I teased back.

"The dishes, amigo." She walked away toward the mess hut. Then she turned back. To my surprise—and delight—she blew me a kiss.

11

R ain showers swept the compound almost every day. As a sudden sprinkle pattered the lab's metal roof, I worked my way along the aquarium rows, warily scraping algae from the interior sides without harm to the occupants—or myself. Then I fed my monsters, concentrating on their welfare, not on the question: to what end? I was paid to study this lethal collection and submit samplings, not to reason why.

The lab door creaked open. Agata stepped in, carrying the mid-morning coffee tray, now with two mugs. My suggestion.

She set the tray on the worktable. "Two mugs, amigo, as you asked."

I had brought another stool from the supply shed—something I had avoided doing for Ted—and we sat together. Sipped coffee. Gazed out into the hazy rain, now falling more heavily.

"I hate the damned rainy season," I muttered.

"Oh, no, amigo. It is so...so..."

I glanced at her. Holding her coffee delicately in the fingertips of both hands, she turned to me with a warm smile. "So intimamente."

I felt a rush of warmth, but it was followed by a wave of apprehension. Civil but not familiar, Emmett. A social convention already erased by seclusion and Felicia's frigid abandonment. Where did I go from here?

"Yes," I murmured. "Intimate."

She set down her mug, stood to reach for the broom. I sat there, stared into the mist-shrouded compound. This forsaken place had eaten up two men before me. Could I be falling into the same disintegration that had sent Warnowski—and possibly Melvin Proctor before him—homeward hollow-eyed and gibbering?

I was barely aware the broom's coarse swish had stopped. To my amazement, I felt her hands rest softly on my shoulders. What was this?

Her fingertips brushed my neck then gently began to massage the tense muscles. I was stunned. Then elated, I touched her caressing fingers.

Together, we had crossed the line.

***

"Tell me about Manaus," I asked her as we finished our supper of roast wild boar bought from the Bororo village, a repast topped off with fried bananas. High living in desolation.

"About your life there." I caught her grimace of distaste. "I mean before that. When you were..."

"More young."

"Yes. More young."

"My pai..."

"Pai?"

"My father. He was good to me. A nice man. He drive trucks for road making. When that stop, he find no more work in Manaus. He go to Colombia. To emerald mine. To send dinhiero to us. A good man but not much money."

"He did send you that pendant, though."

"Sim." She fingered her ever-present pendant. "But I wonder how."

The emerald, assuming it was the real thing, had to be worth major money. She caught my stare at her remarkable gemstone. "Amigo?"

"Agata, with all you've gone through, I can't help wondering why you haven't sold the pendant. That emerald has to be worth a lot of money."

"It is all I have left of my family, amigo." She paused then smiled, a bit craftily, I thought. "If I sell it, a poor working woman, that would be a big news. And I do not need a big news about me."

Best not to push that. "So after he left, what did you do?"

"I stay in school until I, too, have to be a cook. I want to do more. A teacher, meibi, but I have to do what there is to do. I cook. At the restaurant. Then I marry Luis Portel. Not a good man. Muy jealous man. Thinks all the time I look at other men."

I toyed with a spoon. "Did you?"

"Não! But he never believe me."

"And he beat you." This sad, lonely woman. In her delicate face— soft eyes, high cheekbones, lovely lips — there was such potential. All of it suspended by circumstance.

She gave me a quick glance. "I tell you of my family. You tell me of yours?"

"Oh? Not very exciting. My father was a high-school English teacher..."

"Teach English where you speak English?"

"Taught the finer points. Grammar, usage—how to write well. He's retired now. My mother's retired, too. She was manager of a gift shop. Good manager. Both were hard workers. And they were quite demanding."

I saw her confusion.

"They expected much from me."

She brightened. "But they loved you."

"Because they loved me, Agata."

She folded her hands as if she had reached some conclusion. "I must tell you a thing, amigo. For a time, Luis Portel made me hate men. But you...you change that. I owe you big debt. For that and for my freedom."

Freedom? In desolate, jungle-bound Station Four?

"You owe me nothing, Agata."

"I owe you everything." She rose, stacked the dishes and set them in the sink. "Everything," she said over her shoulder. Then she stepped back to the table and gently took my hand. "Por favor," she whispered. "Come with me."

Mystified and intrigued, I followed her through the kitchen then into her small room in the rear of the mess building.

***

The soft light of early evening filtered through the single window's curtain. By Station standards, her room was surprisingly cozy. A sea-green blanket on the netting-tented cot, the small multi-colored woven rug, a fabric wall-hanging all spoke of a spirit brighter than that of a fugitive woman willing to work at menial tasks in this forsaken outback.

I studied the wall hanging more closely. Some sort of rough tan cloth, painted with a riot of symbols and primitive human shapes.

"Fascinating," I murmured. "What is it? Some sort of voodoo painting?"

She laughed, the first time I had heard her truly laugh, a charming musical lilt. "Who knows? I bought in Santarém for the color."

I turned away from the crude artwork—and stared...

"My God, Agata! What in the world..."

"Amigo," she breathed. "Amigo. I owe you so much."

A hot wave of embarrassment engulfed me. Words wouldn't come.

While I'd examined the wall decoration, she'd slipped off her dress. Everything. In the darkening shadows, she stood gloriously nude, a gorgeous sculpture in bronze.

"Agata..." My voice sounded as if I were strangling. "You don't have to do this. You mustn't do this. Anything like this. You owe me nothing."

She stepped close, so close I felt her warmth. "I owe you everything. My liberdade. My vida. You are...mi querido."

"Querido?"

"It is...warmer than 'amigo.'" Her arms reached toward me. "This is all I have to repay you."

"Lord's sake, Agata. I don't need repayment."

"But I must, querido. You have been so kind to me. You lied for me."

I cringed a little at that. But she was right.

She took both my hands in hers. Her touch sent a wash of heat through me. I knew I should resist. I tried to resist. Until I wondered: why? Felicia had walked out. Oliver seemed detached from all that had happened. What was left? This beautiful, yearning woman. Repayment for a lie in her behalf? Might she also be responding to the contrast between her husband's brutality and our warming friendship?

Her dark-tipped breasts brushed my shirt. She had an intoxicating jungle flower scent. And I lost what little control I still had. Willingly. Reached for her. Drew her tight against me. Met her parted lips with mine. I felt her fingers unbutton my shirt. Shuck it off. I yanked away the rest of my clothes.

Scandalous. Sinful. And I didn't give a damn. Felicia hadn't given a damn. Why should I?

We thrust the mosquito net aside, sank to the cot. All these months, who could imagine anything like this lithe woman had been concealed beneath that shapeless tan smock?

Her fingers were a caress as gentle as the touch of tropical fronds, her body warm and soft and sweet. "You are so brando, querido," she murmured.

"Brando?"

"Gentle, I think. But..." Her lips sought mine again, softly, then with stunning insistence. The rain increased to a pounding shower. "Oh, mi querido," she murmured in my ear. "Maravilhoso."

Felicia had been almost inertly compliant. Agata's initial gentleness quickly built into erotic initiative that left me breathless. Then I was gripped by passion I'd never felt before. Fugitive and adulterer locked in lust. Rain pelted the roof in a thunderous downpour. God help us both.

As the shower tapered off, the jungle silence was broken only by our breathing. We lay side by side; then she bent over me, kissed me tenderly. "Thank you, mi querido," she whispered. "Thank you."

Drums, I thought. There should be a throb of distant drums.

***

In the morning's mugginess, I wondered: Who seduced whom? When I invited Agata to share mealtimes with me, the idea of any further itinerary hadn't been even a passing impulse. I had to admit, though, as I vainly tried to concentrate on my work, she had become increasingly attractive through the days following that precedent-shattering breakfast. Now our station chief and cook-housekeeper relationship had become man and woman in the most intimate way. And so unlike Felicia's structured approach to love-making with her rapidly cooling aftermath. Agata had been inspiringly uninhibited. I'd never felt such exhilaration.

How delightfully reckless last night had been! At breakfast, her smile, unmistakably mischievous, said it all. Where, I wondered, will this relationship go now? If her offering herself had been only what she had said it to be — repayment for putting Rolha off the track — I could live with that. I would certainly not go to her, expecting further acquiescence. For an employer, that was unthinkable. Better to treasure the memory of one incredible night and..."carry on."

***

I tried to concentrate on conducting business as usual. Wearing latex gloves, I lifted my six bright yellow dart-poison frogs from their tank one by one, and pinched the hind legs of each until the frog sweated white froth. I collected the deadly stuff in a test tube and scraped the lethal oil beneath it into another, each tube then carefully capped and labeled. These would be part of my next package to Oriximiná via Picos's launch, there to be transferred to a Belém-bound cruise ship. Thence to an international cargo flight to Philadelphia.

As I packed the capped tubes for shipment, I felt Agata and I were each other's rescuers. Me, with the lie concerning her date of arrival here; she with her warmth and intimacy dissolving the pain of Felicia's desertion.

What now? Felicia and Ted were sure to return to Philadelphia, if they weren't already there. That certainty and last night's abandon had slipped my last finger-hold on convention. I felt elated.

I stripped off the protective gloves, dropped them in the metal drum that served as an incinerator behind the lab. Overhead, a transient troupe of monkeys chattered. In the compound's canopy, the monkey's pink ears contrasted with their gray fur. They gibbered southward. Silence closed around me again, so profound it seemed to muffle the river's ever-present burbling. This was, I thought uneasily, the kind of silence that preceded a violent storm.

I stared at the mess hut. As she went about her chores, what was Agata thinking this morning? That she had simply repaid a debt? That she had seduced her employer, thereby gaining a substantial advantage over him? Or was she a desperately lonely woman in need of whatever kind of affection I might offer?

I struck a match, dropped it in the refuse drum. Flame ran along the edge of a discarded carton and licked at the stained gloves. As they began to melt, I stepped back, careful to avoid contact with the toxic smoke.

***

At lunch some days later, she asked me, "What do you need, mi querido?"

"Nothing, Agata. That was a fine meal."

"Não, querido. I mean what do you need?"

Startled, I repeated, "What do I need?" Intriguing question. "A larger generator perhaps, so we could have longer hours of electricity. A shower room. The buildings up on pilings so a bad rainy season won't flood us out. Better lab equipment. More..."

She leaned toward me, now unsmiling. Earnest. Midday heat flooded the mess hut's open door. I heard a bird screech, the distant thuds of a hammer as Jheem and Haree replaced yet another strip of termite-riddled siding on the storage shed. Station Four was at peace, and I knew the honest answer to her question.

"What I need is...you, Agata."

Her face solemn, she nodded. "And I need you, mi querido."

While I tried to recover from that soul-warming exchange, she abruptly stood and began to clear the table.

12

When we began our meals together, I wondered what Agata and I would talk about. There were long silences, but now our chatter came easily. At last, and for the first time in a long time at Station Four, one day flowed seamlessly into the next.

My hair had grown over my collar. Felicia had been my occasional barber; now I asked Agata to take on that task. She handled the scissors deftly. When she finished her shearing, I was intrigued I'd been so neatly — and gently — trimmed by a woman who had stabbed her husband in defensive fury.

One misty afternoon I realized I knew more about Agata as a woman than I'd ever known about Felicia. That jangled my fading conscience but was forgotten by the time Agata joined me at supper. There was something different in her glances tonight — something searching, though she talked only of the persistent rumble of distant thunder.

"To the norte, mi querido. Too much thunder. The full rainy season begins." After a pause, she asked quietly, "The rio, how high does it rise?"

"Last year, it came within four feet of the top of the bank. Gave us a real scare."

"If a flood, where do we go?"

"To higher ground at the storage building. And if the water gets too high for that we leave in the boat. But there's no need to worry about that now."

"Não, amigo." Her eyes softened. "We will think of other things."

***

Did I deserve this? I wondered as I completed salinity checks on the Gulf-puffer fish tanks. Work I liked, though I couldn't help debating its true value. An incredibly warm and understanding woman? This rainforest site that for the first time I could consider exotic? And a question I had found unthinkable until now: Might it be possible next year to renew my contract with the Foundation for another two years?

In the days that followed that incredibly intimate night with Agata, I began to conclude it had been exactly what she said it was: repayment for the debt she owed me. An erotic repayment with no future implication. I felt disappointment, but I forced myself to accept it. To press her for more such intimate generosity was out of the question. I had never been that kind of man—to the disdain of some of my college classmates. In retrospect, I realized, Felicia had most often been the instigator, though her follow-through was uninspired. Had that been a mistake? After our just-married burst of sexual adventuring, we'd lapsed into routine coupling. Had that been a factor in her response to Ted Rebner's hard sell?

Didn't matter now; all in the past. Life at Station Four had become so bearable, I immersed myself in my work, warmed by mealtime conversation with Agata—and the memory of our magic night. Then on a rainy evening a week or so after that incredible experience, as we finished our roast pork and fried plantain supper, she reached across the table to touch my hand gently.

"Stay," she whispered. "I do dishes later."

I felt a surge of excitement. Ready in an instant. She smiled, threw down her dishtowel, and we hurried to her little bedroom behind the kitchen.

Was she giving herself this second time because I hadn't pressed her? She'd mentioned her loneliness more than once, had spoken of my "niceness" to her. Was that all it took for this mistreated woman to offer me such abandon? Happily confused, I decided to stop trying to rationalize as a scientist and enjoy my good fortune as a man.

Slowly this time, languidly, I kissed each bronze breast and explored until she trembled. Then we were lost in each other. Ecstasy in the jungle. I was both elated and distressed that I could be falling in love with this woman.

She proved uncanny in her ability to recognize the point where I felt these evening interludes were finally over. She would gently touch the back of my hand with her warm fingertips, and I would be instantly afire with anticipation. Smart woman. I would never be sated with her as I now acknowledged I had become with Felicia during her lush jungle resurgence.

How long had she and Ted been gone? A month? Only that? Already they seemed part of a distant past, a memory fast-fading in the vibrant new awareness Agata had given me.

I added my puffer tank observations to my meticulous notations and returned the notebook to its work-shelf drawer. Then I paused. Heard a distant chuffing. Stepped into the soggy compound and scanned the river. Picos? He wasn't due until next week.

Picos indeed. His ancient launch nosed around the river's south bend and plowed toward the Station. In minutes, gray smoke drifted over the riverbank. I heard the hiss of vented steam and voices down at the dock. To my astonishment, a woman in loosely fitted khaki slacks, a long-sleeved blue shirt and a floppy straw sun hat stepped onto the dock. Picos handed her a tote bag, and she climbed up the riverbank's crest.

My God. Felicia. I was so stunned I didn't know what to say. Obviously, neither did she. As she strode past me, I got only a tense little nod.

Eyes fixed ahead, she walked straight to our residence door, pulled it open, stepped in and shut it behind her.

I walked back to the lab and sat on the lab stool, stunned. Her returning wasn't the last thing I expected. I hadn't considered it at all. I was flabbergasted. Then I was panicked. What would she deduce from Agata's appearance in a bright flowered dress? Her glossy hair cascading to her shoulders?

I couldn't just sit here in confusion. I pushed out of the lab and trotted back to the riverbank.

"Hola!" Picos shouted from the dock.

"Will you join me for coffee, Capitán?" I called. I found myself hoping his bouncy presence might help cover my consternation at Felicia's bewildering "homecoming."

"Muchas gracias, señor, but not today. I must make trip down to Obidos before the river, she gets too high." He swung an arm toward the water. "It is up already a half meter. Ay, Juan," he called to his deckhand, "cast off."

The launch drifted free of the dock. Smoke belched from its battered stack. "Back nex' time with the gas," I heard Picos shout. "If river not too high." The steam engine's chuffing increased its tempo. The grubby little launch swung away in a wide southward turn and disappeared around the bend.

From the riverbank, I stared into the Trombetas without seeing it. Felicia's stunning return left me with a feeling of desolation. She was here, but did I want her here? I had lost her to Ted Rebner, and now, through her unanticipated presence, I knew I had lost Agata.

I faced the most difficult challenge I had ever faced. I walked to the residence door, grasped the latch. Hesitated. Then I opened the door and stepped in.

She hunched on the edge of her cot, knees tight together, head in her hands. I perched on my cot. I didn't know what to say.

"Felicia, I..."

She looked up, eyes wet with tears. As if she had no strength left, her hands fell to her lap. "Oh, God, Emmett," she sobbed, "I'm so ashamed. So sorry. Can you ever forgive me?"

My question as well, I realized. I was shocked at her appearance. She had lost her lush tropical metamorphosis and reverted to the angular bony woman she had been on our arrival here. Her caramel hair hung limp around her pale face. Her hands wouldn't stop fidgeting.

"What brought you back, Felicia? I thought you had gone for...good." I could have made a better word choice, but I was picking my way through a whirl of confusion.

"Idiot," she muttered.

"Who?"

"Ted. I don't know why I didn't see that sooner. A total idiot. A whiner. In the hospital, he behaved abominably. A thirty-year-old with teenage mentality. I was ashamed of him. And of myself—for being such a stupid, stupid... My God, who am I to talk about his teenage mentality?"

"Felicia, you don't have to do this."

"I do have to, Emmett. I do. You may never forgive me, but I want you to know how I feel now. Like an ugly little tramp, Emmett. I can't imagine how I let myself do what I did."

The isolation. I could almost hear Warnowski's hollow rasp.

"Well," I finally managed, "You're here now. And he's...just where in hell is he, Felicia?"

"Still at the hospital. Uncle Oliver has guaranteed all expenses. So Teddy is lapping up the attention. Moaning and groaning through rehab."

"It was his hip?"

"Yes. Pretty bad, but I could see he was milking it for all it was worth."

"That can't go on forever. What does he plan to do next?"

"Ted doesn't plan anything. Oliver has ordered him back to Philadelphia as soon as he's fit to travel."

And good riddance. Now, guilty as she was, what should I say? Two adulterers in this garden of exile.

So I said, "Have you had anything to eat today?"

"Coffee and toast in Oriximiná, courtesy of Captain Picos."

"You need more than that." I stood.

"Wait, Emmett. There's something more I must tell you. I...I owe you such a huge apology."

"I thought you already made it, Felicia." That came out unintentionally snide. I was in real conflict. She had betrayed me. But hadn't I betrayed her?

"I mean about the... In Belém I had a lot of time to think. I replayed Ted's fall down the bank over and over. What I saw of it. Step by step in slow motion. I can still see it. But now I got to the point where I wasn't sure what I saw. When it happened, I believed what he told me. I looked out our window and saw him showing off with some strange kind of...I don't know. A clumsy little jig. What was that all about?"

"You didn't see him knock me down?"

"He knocked you down?"

"In a fit of anger, I rushed at him. He slapped me on the head and I tripped and went down. He was so delighted with his triumph, he broke into that goofy jig. Just as I was getting back on my feet, he lost his balance. I made a dive for him. Too late."

She looked down at the floor, then up at me. Eyes now so sad I said nothing.

"When I saw you rush at him..."

"I was trying to save him from falling, Felicia, not push him."

"In my heart, I knew you couldn't have pushed him, Emmett. But God help me, I believed him. He kept harping that you did until I couldn't bear to be near him any longer."

I fought back a told-you-so impulse.

"Emmett? Please."

I let out a long breath. "It was a trauma for all of us. But now you've gotten it straight. I absolutely did not shove Ted down the bank."

"I know. Now I know. But he's convinced himself you did. He hates you, Emmett."

"Doesn't matter now." I pushed up from the cot.

She looked up, forlorn. I bent down, kissed her forehead. Her forehead? I just couldn't get myself to offer a warm embrace.

"Let's get something to eat," I suggested. A way to end her painful confessions.

Halfway across the compound, it hit me again. Christ, when she saw Agata all decked out in vacation mode, hair flying free...

"Maybe it's a little early for lunch," I said. A feeble attempt to delay the inevitable.

"I thought you were hungry, Emmett."

We strode on, ever nearer the mess hut, where I knew my already rattled life was about to be forever unglued. I opened the door for her, peered in. Agata was not in sight. Then I heard her stepping out of her room. I tensed.

"Ah, Senhora Durkin," Agata said with a smile. "Boa tarde. Lunch, Senhor Durkin?" Shapeless in her ankle-length muumuu, her hair in a tight bun, she turned to the stove.

"Whatever you can put together for us, Agata, will be fine."

I felt I had been reprieved from a bleak future, if any future at all.

13

Agata had skillfully reverted to her former housekeeper-cook subservience. Felicia exuded an aura of contriteness. I struggled with myself. Talk about conflict. Should my guilt over my intimate relationship with Agata cancel the impact of Felicia's lapse with Ted? How long, I wondered, would Agata stay with her apparent resignation to Felicia's unexpected return? I did notice her occasional quick smile at me—when she knew Felicia would not see it. Did she feel the same sense of loss I was struggling with? Despite her serene demeanor in our presence, I wondered if fervor still simmered in her little room behind the kitchen.

On the surface, life at Station Four returned almost to its pre-Ted routine. Quiet breakfasts in the mess shack's haven from the cloying rainy-season mist. Lab work, with Agata still bringing my mid-morning coffee, but now with only one mug on the tray. I was impressed by her flawless return to impersonal servant status. At the same time, I was disappointed she could so easily dispose of what I had felt was a close, warm relationship.

I studied my bubbling tanks, the unsavory specimens within, wondered what in hell value all this had—other than serving as a fund-raising "glamour" project. Then I shrugged off such cynicism, opened my notebook and...carried on.

***

The almost daily showers became more intense. Following a conversationally-strained lunch, several days after Felicia's return, I stood on the crest of the bank, arms folded, lips compressed. The Trombetas flowed significantly higher. Up some three feet in the past few days, leaving only fifteen feet of the bank above water level. This had to be the fastest increase since we'd arrived here a year and a half ago. The floating dock, with the Whaler secured to its upstream side, had risen with the water level, of course. Now the dock floated even with its two retaining stakes.

As I stared at the river, I saw a thick branch from a fallen tree upriver drift around the north bend. The strong current carried the branch downstream — and shoreward. I stood there numb, frustrated with my inability to do a damned thing about its ominous approach. As if it were on a programmed course, the branch headed straight for the upstream side of the dock. I winced as the butt end crunched into the Whaler's portside. The branch pivoted, its leafed end pulling it free to resume its rapid downstream drift.

A wave of hot anger swept through me, anger at my own ineptness. I had just witnessed what I should have envisioned weeks ago. I scrambled halfway down the bank to where I could get a good look at the Whaler's portside. I knew Whalers did not sink. Cut into three sections, even the portion with the engine would float, according to one of their dramatic ads. But a leaking hull could fill the boat with water to the gunwales, making it unmanageable.

I could see the branch had dented the fiberglass, but the hull did not appear fractured. We needed to shelter the boat from further floating debris. I decided to move it to the downstream side of the dock. I rushed back to the residence for the key. Might need some help on this, I decided. I found Jheem working on a leak in the mess shack's roof. He scrambled down, loped to the residence and reappeared from behind it with Haree in tow. The three of us raced to the bank, plunged down. I rolled back the Whaler's cover and set it on the dock. Stepped aboard, lowered the outboard engine until the prop was submerged. I planned to push into the current at about a 45-degree angle, then turn downriver, pass the dock 100 feet or so offshore. A final 270-degree turn to port would loop me shoreward angling against the current, heading for the dock's downriver side where, with the Bororos' help, we would re-secure the mooring lines.

I twisted the key. The engine stuttered. Popped. Gave it another try. No go. Water in the gas? A clogged gas line? I could work on that later. The immediate problem was to move the boat to the downriver side of the dock.

Plan B. I stepped back onto the wet boards, freed the Whaler's wet, slippery aft-line. Tossed it to the Bororos. Jumped to the bowline, freed it from the dock cleat, tugged it hard with both hands.

"Need slack!" I shouted to my two guys. Not in their limited English vocab, but they knew what I meant. They stepped toward me, both of them pulling fiercely on the sleek line, Jheem with one hand on the rope, the other shoving the boat's stern. I strained at the bowline. Pressed into the dock by the strong current, the Whaler inched along. When we managed to get the boat nosed halfway beyond the dock, the current caught it with a vengeance. I stepped backward to take up the sudden slack in the bowline.

Jheem and Haree abruptly had the opposite problem. The current rammed the Whaler around the dock's corner to head downstream. The aft line sprang taut in the Bororos' hands. Jheem stumbled, fell to his knees. The hard yank on the aft-line pulled it from his grasp. Haree, still gripping the line, lunged forward and fell flat on his belly, still clutching the line.

I backpedaled frantically, trying to haul the bow against the dock's forward edge. But now the current caught the boat from aft. The stern swung wide, dragging Haree toward the dock's forward edge. As he bounced off the Station's overturned canoe, Jheem lunged for the line, got one hand on it, but our cause was lost. I grabbed his shoulder, looked back at Haree. Shrugged hopelessly. Made a hand-opening gesture to both of them.

"Let go!" I shouted. "Let go before you're both pulled off the dock."

The three of us watched the Whaler swirl away in the irresistible current. It swung wide around the south bend. And was gone.

I stood there stunned, the world's stupidest skipper. Lost my boat through lack of smarts. One way of putting it. A more honest way would be to confess I had been too occupied with Agata to consider the boat's vulnerability. And a few other things.

One of them was the security of the canoe — and the dock itself. I had Jheem and Haree carry the canoe and its two paddles to the top of the bank. They leaned it against a nearby tree and would come back later to lash it and the paddles to the tree trunk.

Moving the dock stakes took a while. We uprooted the downstream stake, relocated it higher on the bank as the taut new upstream line. Unhitched the original upstream line and moved it and its stake into position as the slack downstream line. That done, and with the stakes now located several yards higher than the dock, we climbed the weedy bank to its crest, all of us panting in the dismal afternoon.

My heart sinking, I stood at the bank's crest and looked at the faded green canoe. If the Station flooded out, the Bororos could retreat to their village. Could Felicia, Agata and I trust ourselves to this tippy canoe aswirl in the river's rushing current? Might we be better off following Jheem and Haree to their village — if they would have us and if the village itself had not gone under?

What was I thinking? Had we not survived last year's rainy season right here at Station Four?

***

The end of each month was payday for Jheem and Haree. The Foundation had set up bank accounts in Santarém for Agata and me, with our salaries deposited monthly. Capitán Picos was paid per trip by Foundation check. The Bororos were paid by me in Foundation-supplied cash, each with a small stack of reals. I had wondered what use cash would be in a remote Trombetas village. But following each payday, I noticed several dugouts heading south. To Oriximiná, I deduced, to buy goods the rainforest did not provide.

I kept the cash fund in a steel strongbox in the residence with the key on the ring in my pocket. After our ill-fated dock effort, I paid Jheem and Haree and returned the strongbox key to my pocket. By long-standing custom, the Bororos had the rest of payday off. They trotted away, and I spent the balance of the afternoon in the lab's soggy solitude, forcing myself through the dissection of a Gulf puffer. I didn't enjoy dissections: reducing a living creature to organic debris in quest of lethal venom and organ samples for shipment to Philadelphia.

Supper was no easier. Felicia picked at her black beans and rice.

"I radioed Picos about our fugitive boat," I said into the silence.

"Chances are?" Felicia asked without looking up from her plate.

"Barring sheer luck, I'd guess chances are nil to none. Too many hazards. Bashed to pieces by flood debris. Found by someone claiming salvage rights, or just keeps his mouth shut. We'll never see it again."

And that was the extent of our dinner conversation. We could not go on like this. Felicia sensed that too. And as we prepared for bed in the damp residence, she abruptly said, "Emmett, we simply must come to some sort of, well, truce between us. I can't keep facing day after day of not knowing whether our marriage has been destroyed — or that we might try to work out some sort of…" Her voice trailed off.

"I know. And I've come to a conclusion."

She looked devastated. "A conclusion?"

"Yep. It's this. I put my hands on her shoulders and looked into her aqua eyes. I said it slowly: "Felicia, there is no past." This had to be the resolution of Felicia's fling with Teddy, I knew — and to my eager lapses with Agata. Blank out all of it. There was no past.

"No past?" Her anguish had reduced her to echoes.

I took her in my arms. "None," I said. "We go on from here. Together."

"Oh, Emmett," she sighed, and her tension melted against me. I kissed her. With feeling.

"No past," she whispered.

I felt as liberated as I sensed did she. She smiled, touched my lips lightly, and sat on her cot then lay back with a little sigh.

"Edge over a bit." I stretched out beside her, touched her breast beneath her pajama top. "A kiss is not enough."

In the glow of the room's single bulb, I noticed color had returned to her pale cheeks. Her hair had regained a good bit of its former luster. Then up in the supply shed, the generator cut out on schedule. Our lonely bulb faded to an orange glow then died. We welcomed the darkness. And each other. I held her close, but she stunned me by pulling away. I was dismayed. Until I realized she was stripping off her pajamas. I was unexpectedly elated. I shed my own PJs, not easy on the narrow cot, arms and legs flailing. In a rush of relief—and anticipation—I took her back in my arms.

"Oh God, Emmett," she whispered, "I'm so ashamed. I know now I loved you even through my whole stupid..."

"Shh, Felicia. There is no past." I took her with an urgency that surprised us both.

Equanimity had returned to Station Four.

For less than a week.

14

Iglanced up from my notebook. An airplane? It roared low over the station. I rushed outside. Jheem, working on a siding repair at the east end of the residence, also stared.

A seaplane, now racing across the river. Chunky fuselage, big radial engine, bright red wings. The Santarém Norseman emergency plane. But I hadn't radioed for any such response.

The plane crossed the Trombetas, banked through a one-eighty turn over the river's far shore, then glided to a smooth landing on the flowing water. What was this? I hurried to the riverbank.

The pilot let the plane drift southward about a quarter mile; then the idling engine barked power. The Norseman taxied toward the Station, angling against the current. The pilot deftly edged the big plane to the dock's downriver side. Exactly what I had intended to do with our Whaler before it broke away. The plane's forward door popped open. Holding a coiled line, the chunky co-pilot stepped down on the starboard float, secured it to a dock cleat. The propeller still flipped over. I figured they weren't here for long.

The co-pilot reached up, opened the passenger compartment door. A man in rumpled suntans emerged awkwardly, his foot fumbling for the little metal loop below the door. The co-pilot grabbed his passenger's ankle to guide him. The clumsy passenger shook off the help. The co-pilot stuck the foot in place anyway. I sensed he'd had enough of this unappreciative debarker. The passenger eased down on the dock. Stumbled. Again, he shook off the offered arm. Scowling, the airman reached back into the passenger section, pulled out a lumpy travel bag. He offered to help the hobbling man up the bank. Was refused again. The co-pilot shrugged, dropped the bag at his passenger's feet, stepped back on the float, retrieved his line, shoved his foot against the dock edge and climbed back aboard.

In the current, the plane drifted away from shore. The pilot fed in power and the big Norseman turned eastward, plowed across the river's swollen water, swung around into the west wind. The plane rose up on the step before the engine's roar reached me. The Norseman lifted, climbed, racketed straight overhead then faded away to the southwest.

Ted Rebner had returned. Regardless of the hobble, I could have deduced that from his attitude alone. I stood there watching him hitch sideways up the bank. He didn't want help, and I didn't offer any. His determination was that of a man with a mission. A chill broke across my shoulders.

When he struggled almost to the crest, sweating and panting, I was stunned by his gaunt, sunken-eyed appearance. Despite his sullen expression, I nodded.

"Welcome back, Ted," I said as he topped the bank." I tried to sound off-hand, but it came out as sarcasm.

"Where's the Whaler?"

"The current took it. I doubt we'll ever see it again." I motioned downhill. "You left your bag on the dock."

He looked down as if I'd made that up just to bug him. Then he yelled at Jheem, "You! Go get my bag."

"You," I snapped at Ted, "do not order my people to do anything."

Jheem, beginning to trot toward us, stopped. Eyes on me.

"Jheem," I called, "por favor." I pointed. "Bring up his bag."

When he clambered down then back up with the damned bag, Ted grabbed it. Without a word of thanks, he pushed past me in his lurching gait and headed for the residence as if he had a confirmed reservation.

"Dinner in an hour," I called after him.

No response.

***

"Was that an airplane I heard this afternoon?" Felicia settled into her mess shack camp chair. "I was asleep. Woke me up. It sounded like it flew over us twice."

"You missed the return of the prodigal son...of a bitch."

Her face froze. "Ted's come back? But he told me his uncle told him to go back to Philadelphia."

"Who knows what evil lurks...?" I murmured. My attention was on Ted, hitching across the compound toward us. Now that all eyes could be on him, he appeared to be limping noticeably more than when he arrived.

He banged the screen door open and sank into the chair across from me, his eyes hard on mine.

"This is a surprise, Ted," Felicia chirped. "I thought you were heading straight home from Belém."

"I have unfinished business here."

"You have no business here, Ted, unless you want to do your share of the work."

I slapped margarine on a slice of bread and took an angry bite. "Unfinished business. Christ."

Ted's eyes burned with what looked to me like hatred.

"Damn it, Ted, if you've convinced yourself I shoved you down that bank, you are sadly…"

"I know what happened, Durkin. Felicia knows what happened. And I…"

"For heavens sake, Ted!" Felicia broke in. "I was mistaken. You fell all on your own."

He swung back to me. "You've worked on her, haven't you? I don't care what she thinks now. I know what happened and I'm not leaving here until I…"

What was left of my patience gave way. "For God's sake, Ted, shut up. Eat your supper."

He shot me a smile that held no humor at all. "I'll do what the hell I want, Durkin…. What I came back to do."

I'm his unfinished business? I thought with a near-shudder. But I said, "Eat."

In the silence that followed, Agata padded between kitchen and dining table, her bronze face impassive. But her eyes kept returning to Ted. Eyes hard as glass.

"Fish!" he growled. A switch in repugnance from me to his dinner. "Fish in the hospital, fish on the Belém-Santarém boat. Now it's fish here."

May you choke on a bone, I hoped. An unworthy impulse, but even his boorish reaction to our menu ratcheted my apprehension up another notch.

"I am sorry, Senhor Rebner," Agata said without sounding sorry at all. "I will see what can be done."

"God damned fish," Ted fumed. But he ate it anyway.

"You heard from my uncle?" he asked me, his words muffled by his mouthful.

"You mean in reference to you?"

"Yeah. I assume you wired him right after it happened."

"I did, and he wired back."

"So what did he say?"

I found satisfaction in relaying Oliver's cryptic response. "He said, 'Carry on.'"

"Carry on? What the hell does that mean?"

"I assume it means just what he said."

"Nothing about me?"

I smiled. "Not a word about you. But I understand he did contact you in the hospital."

"Ordered me home. Nobody orders me. And I'm not going anywhere until I...until I'm finished here."

I compressed my lips. No sense making this worse. No one said another word as Agata brought in a dessert platter of plantains fried in brown sugar.

Last to leave the mess shack, I was unable to resist a long look back at Agata. Her eyes met mine. If I expected to find resignation in her expression, it was not there. The set of her jaw told me she did not, after all, intend to revert so docilely to her role as station menial. I found that exhilarating. And disturbing.

***

In the clammy morning, Felicia and I watched Ted gobble down scrambled eggs Agata had just acquired from the arriving Bororos, fried pork, toast and Agata's rich Arabica coffee.

"Three this morning," he said as he set down his mug. A fleck of egg decorated his chin stubble.

"Three what, Ted?" Felicia's fluttery bright tone told me she was beginning to realize we could be dealing with a seriously warped man.

"Push-ups. I could do only one the day I left Belém. Push-ups for progress." He didn't smile.

Jesus, push-ups for progress! That told me something. I wondered at what push-up goal Ted would feel ready to progress to what he had come back to do? Twenty? Fifteen? Maybe only ten.

"I think that's wonderful, Ted." Again, that jolly I-could-be-dealing-with-a-nut tone. "Don't you think so, Emmett?"

I pushed back my chair. "I've got to get to the lab."

Narrowly getting out of the mess shack before I blew up, I sat on the lab stool facing the aquarium array, elbows on the work shelf behind me. I loved this work—and hated it. Loved the controlled danger of my wards; hated chopping them up for their venomous specimens. Not the eel, of course. He was an old timer, in residence when Felicia and I arrived. As were the stingrays, also survivors of Warnowski's neglect. Through the past year and a half, I'd received shipped-in replacements for the species he'd let die of inattention, and shipments of several new deadly denizens of the deep. The most recent had arrived, via Picos, just after our bleak Christmas. Two bulky, water-filled, environmentally secure Styrofoam boxes. A dozen Synanceja horrida, warty spiny-finned stonefish from the Philippines. And, from the Mediterranean Sea, sixteen small Trachinus draco, greater weeverfish with spiny dorsal and ventral fins almost the full length of their slender bodies.

During my months-ago conducted tour of the lab for new arrival Ted's benefit, he had walked out. If he stuck his nose in now with some sense of curiosity, I would take great pleasure in watching him blanch over the ability of the mud-colored stonefish's dorsal spines to inflict instant shooting pains, not fatal but incapacitating for several hours. The weeverfish's needle-sharp dorsal spines also produced instant pain, a torment that would spread to an almost unendurable peak in a half hour. The excruciating agony lasted a full day. Without prompt treatment, the victim could suffer gangrene, even die from the sting. My stonefish and weeverfish were juveniles now, but when they reached maturity, I would — to my distaste — have to extract their venom.

Ted, because you didn't give a damn, you missed the newest stars in my show.

I'd been at work twenty minutes when to my surprise, he appeared. At the entrance, he stumbled and grabbed the doorjamb's two-by-four for support.

"Still futzing around with your chamber of horrors, I see."

I glanced up from my measuring the voltage output of the Electrophorus eel. "That's why we're here. Too bad you've never realized that." I shook my head in impatience then tried for a conciliatory tone. "Why don't you do something about your appearance, Ted? You look like a homeless person."

"You think I call this place home? I am a homeless person." Favoring his bad hip, he leaned against the work shelf. "We both know why I was sent to this God-forsaken outpost." To my surprise, he sounded almost self-deprecating. Maybe there was a gleam of hope in that scraggly head.

"I do, indeed. For essentially the same reason you got yourself into major trouble here." I turned back to the big tank. "Why didn't you go back to Philadelphia while you were in Belém? Like your uncle asked."

He was silent for a long, disquieting moment. Then he spoke in no more than a murmur. "I have unfinished business here, Turkey."

From mundane to menace. My knuckles went white on the eel tank's rim. I forced a bantering tone I didn't feel. "Don't stay on my account."

"It is on your account."

I looked at him over my shoulder. For the moment, I needn't fear this wreck hunched against the work shelf. What slithered a tremor down my spine was his intensity.

I straightened. "Why don't you leave what has passed in the past, Ted? Don't exacerbate this unfortunate situation."

"Jesus, Durkin, spare me the academic lingo. I think you're trying to tell me I should accept tit for tat. Well, let me tell you something, you miserable little bastard. It's not the first time a man's wife got interested in somebody who's a lot more of a man. Happens all the time. That's the 'tat.' But your 'tit' has been a hundred times worse than my 'tat.' And, you stuffy little prick —" he slapped his bad hip —"it's permanent."

"So you're up to three push-ups." I moved on to the next tank.

He stood unsteadily. "It's not ended. You can bet your skinny little ass it's not." He lurched out the entrance, slamming the screen door behind him.

I couldn't restrain myself. "Stay out of my lab!" I shouted after him, realizing that surely was not the way to deal with a man on the edge.

Or maybe already over it.

***

At lunch and supper, Ted and I spoke only when it was unavoidable. Felicia, to my surprise, chattered on almost gaily. An attempt to deal with the man's threatening instability, I realized, and perhaps a desperate try to soften the brittle atmosphere?

In the humid bedtime darkness, I tried to concentrate on station business. This afternoon, I'd noticed the river had risen another foot, evidence of downpours to the north. I would have to make certain Jheem and Haree kept a close eye on our floating dock.

Felicia's voice drifted out of the darkness. "I don't know why we can't convince Ted he's so wrong."

"The man is a sociopath, Felicia. Cares for nobody but himself, and he's aggressive about it. There's no reasoning with him. His own lie has convinced him I threw him down the damned bank. He's a scary case of 'I know what I know. Don't confuse me with facts.'"

A long rumble of thunder rattled the roof's corrugated metal. The spatter of the first fat drops of yet another rainfall accelerated to a roar. With luck, Capitán Picos would appear once more until the rainy season subsided. Then we would be stranded here, a mutilated man bordering on dementia. An unfaithful wife in abject remorse. A lusty native mistress suddenly deposed. And myself, an insecure Station chief who had delighted in sleeping with my housekeeper.

Four of us trapped in a forest-ringed island of emotional wreckage. A long roll of thunder jarred the residence.

There should be drums, I thought again. There should be drums.

15

Just after dawn, I jolted awake. Rain pelted the residence roof. Flat on my back, I stared up at the naked trusses supporting the noisy metal roof sheeting. I wondered if the Station would ever return to the tranquility I felt when Picos's launch, Warnowski slumped aboard, chuffed out of sight around the river's south bend and peaceful silence wrapped the compound. I'd looked forward to unhurried days of lab work and easy Station management. A relaxing two-year sojourn in the seclusion of the rainforest. God, how that expectation had been demolished.

The hopeless oaf foisted on us by my employer disrupted my marriage, accused me of criminal assault, and now threatened me personally. I expected—hoped—he was nothing worse than a noisy inert object.... Until acted upon by an external force? Nobody here was about to supply that force. So mutter on, Teddy. Get it all out of your pathetic system.

Abruptly, the rain's drumming increased to a roar. The river. I pushed off the cot, dressed in a hurry. Yanked a yellow slicker over my slacks and shirt. Hurried to the riverbank. A half-mile out, the rapid drift of an entire tree told me the current had again increased. Across the Trombetas, ragged clouds scudded low over the crowns of the upper canopy and its emergent trees. On this side, gusts shivered the water surface.

What was that, a quarter-mile out? I craned forward. A pig-sized agouti, probably washed out of a swollen creek upstream, struggled shoreward. But the big rodent drifted relentlessly downstream, then out of sight around the south bend.

Every year, the Amazon and its tributaries inundated miles of adjacent land. Our remote backwater would soon feel the rainy season's full effect. Mountain storms in upper Para would cascade ever-heavier run-offs down the Trombetas. The glutted Amazon could choke on the outflow and back up far into the rainforest.

I turned away from the sliding expanse and slogged through the compound's yielding softness to the mess hut. Hung my slicker on a nail and sank into my camp chair. Agata already had a pan sizzling on the stove. Despite my apprehension, the tantalizing aroma of frying bacon made me realize how hungry I was.

I glanced across the compound. Not a sign of activity over there.

"Agata?"

"Sim, Senhor?" She turned toward me, spatula in hand.

"I'm...so sorry. I didn't expect either of them to come back."

That sounded sadly inadequate, but I had never...well, broken off an affair before. Never had an affair before. Affair? I guessed that was what it had been, but what an inadequate term. What Agata and I had shared was indefinable. Something...mystical? Now it was gone.

"Of all persons," Agata said softly, "I am last to have anger for a man who returns to the wife he thought lost."

"Agata, you are..." my throat thickened, "you are a remarkable woman."

She set down the spatula, stepped close and gently touched my arm. "Senhor Rebnor you must watch. With much care."

"I appreciate your concern, but I don't think..."

"He means to kill you."

"He's all talk, Agata. Besides, in his condition he couldn't kill a fly."

"That can change."

"Yes, it can. His body gets stronger, but not his brain."

Her fingers squeezed my arm gently. "That is what I fear, mi querido."

"And I appreciate your concern, Agata." I slipped my hand over hers. "I truly do."

Despite my try at reassuring Agata, I was living with apprehension like a persistent ache. How many push-ups now, Ted? I forced myself to concentrate my immediate attention on a mug of hot coffee.

Ten minutes later, Ted clumped in. "Eleven today," he rasped. His color had deepened from pasty white to near-human flesh tone. My uneasiness ratcheted up a notch.

I rushed through potato pancakes and bacon while he sat back and dined in regal silence. Bolting the rest of my coffee, I escaped to the lab.

***

Rain swept along the river in milky sheets and drummed the lab's roof. Hunched on my work-shelf stool with Agata's broom swishing behind me, I glanced at the residence. Felicia had appeared for breakfast after I left. Now, she was back in the residence, no doubt transported from this dismal scene by one of the romance paperbacks Picos delivered by the occasional bagful. Or perhaps she worked on her growing collection of pencil sketches. Ted was... What in hell did he do, other than his infernal push-ups?

As he sweated toward some unannounced goal, I tried to be convinced by a conclusion of my own. Last night I told Felicia, "He's reveling in threats, but I doubt he's thought beyond that. Twenty push-ups? Thirty? He can keep that going indefinitely, wrapped up in his own cleverness."

"I hope you're right, Emmett. But his damned daily announcements are really getting under my skin."

"He's a fraud, Felicia. I'm just about convinced he's all talk without somebody to push him into something more drastic. And nobody here is going to do that."

Without expression, she repeated, "I hope you're right."

"But...?"

"Yes. But."

With that, the generator had cut out, and our conversation died in last night's darkness.

Now, isolated in the lab with Agata's broom swishing rhythmically at the far end, I let myself drift back to those all-too-brief days when we had only each other's company. Days of warmth and passion. Bronze tenderness. Bronze heat.

I swung around. Not sweeping now, she stood at the Gulf-puffer tank. Sphaeroides annulatus. The daring gourmet's delicacy with the added piquancy of sudden death, were the chef careless. Agata stared into the tank. Then sensing my eyes on her, she turned toward me with a look of determination.

"It would be so fácil. So easy."

"No, Agata."

"He wants you dead, mi querido."

"He makes threats, but he's a man of talk, not action."

"That is what I thought of Luis, mi marido."

"I will handle Senhor Rebner, Agata." Easy to say. But how?

I turned back to the work shelf and the dismal vista of the saturated compound. What was Ted doing over there now? Reading a book he might have brought from Belém? Writing a bitchy letter to Uncle Oliver to be relayed by Picos's launch the next time it appeared? Or relentlessly practicing his goddam push-ups? Whatever he did, Ted never showed his face until mealtimes, an intimidating houseguest who refused to pitch in but never missed a meal.

The rush of rain overhead faded to a patter, then quit altogether. To my surprise—and delight, the compound was suddenly bathed in sunlight. An omen, I hoped.

I opened my notebook. Picked up my pen and set to work. Fifteen minutes later—BAM!

What in hell was that! Then two more. From the direction of the residence. What in God's name...

I prided myself on unflappability under duress, but now I threw down my pen, banged open the screen door and ran into the bright mid-morning sunlight. Jheem and Haree piled out of the storage building, dashing faster than I, slapping up water fans. I caught a glimpse of Felicia peering from her doorway as I raced behind the Bororos around the west end of the residence.

I didn't know what to expect, but I felt a sick sensation in my gut. The Bororos stopped suddenly. I pushed past them. I was stunned by what I saw. Ted, his face shaded by his ridiculous Anzac hat, stood over a beautiful Drymarchon corais—beautiful except that its head was shattered. My heart stuttered. Then I was caught up in a wave of hot fury.

"You goddam son of a bitch! You just killed Indy."

He looked at me, totally unimpressed by my boiling anger. And shrugged. "What the hell is 'Indy'?"

"Station Four's resident indigo, you asshole."

He burst into laughter. "Jesus, Turkey, that's the best you can do? A snake for a pet? Lucky I got that damned thing before it got me! I was going out to the crapper, and here was this ten-foot long killer waiting to nail me."

"For God's sake, you idiot. He wasn't about to 'nail' you." Struggling for control, I stared sadly at the six-foot-long, glossy black snake, no doubt emerging to enjoy the unexpected warmth, now undulating in death reflex. "That's one of the most peaceful snakes in the world. The same compliant snake photographers drape over Florida tourists."

Felicia rushed around the corner of the residence. "What happened?" She spotted the decapitated snake. "Oh, my God, Emmett! That's Indy."

"Our great white hunter just slew our friendly indigo."

"I hate snakes!" Ted yipped.

Jheem and Haree still stood a few yards away from the scene of the...crime, damn it. I noticed their faces were not as impassive as usual. Concern over Indy's slaughter perhaps? And over Ted's and my white-hot reactions? I motioned to them and pointed at Indy's remains.

The two Indians stepped in to dispose of Ted's kill. I turned away in disgust. Then the greater significance of the incident hit me.

Ted had a gun.

16

Back in the lab, now a refuge as much as a workplace, I was surprised at how depressed I felt over the loss of Indy. All he offered during his occasional appearances were long, blinkless stares. No eyelids, of course; he couldn't blink. Unless they were about to attack, snakes were expressionless. But Indy... Come on, Emmett. Get on with the Station's pressing challenge: Ted's hatred now escalated even higher.

How, I wondered, did I cope with a brainless lummox bent on revenge, and now armed with a pistol? I couldn't just sit here hoping for the best while we all could be facing the worst.

Anger began to supplement shock. I had to confront this lout.

The compound appeared to have returned to its uneasy normalcy. I forced myself to walk back to the west end of the residence. The sun had faded behind a dense overcast. Our moment of brightness had been shattered by this gun-happy nitwit.

I banged on Ted's door.

The door flew open as if he'd been standing behind it with his hand on the latch, waiting for me. "What the hell do you want?"

"I don't permit firearms here. Give me your damned gun."

"Screw you, Durkin. I make my own rules."

I looked past him. The gun lay in pieces on the floor. "A problem?" I hoped.

"Problem?" He snorted. "I'm cleaning it. I can see you don't know a damned thing about guns. Surplus U.S. Army forty-five," he lectured proudly. "You can buy anything at Bélem's Mercado Sábado."

With Uncle Oliver's air-fare money, no doubt.

"Whatever it is," I said, "I don't want it here. Hand it over."

Another derisive snort. "Not going to happen, Turkey. Before the snake, I already had a good reason to have it." With a grunt, he crouched awkwardly, favoring his bad hip, to fiddle with the spread out gun parts.

I stood over him. "There was no excuse for what you did out there. That was a completely harmless reptile. Beneficial, actually. You had no need to kill it. No damned need at all."

"It was a snake. That's reason enough for me."

I took a deep breath. "Look, Ted. You're an educated man...of sorts. Your uncle wrote that you have a degree in hotel management."

"So?"

"So why don't you get yourself back to civilization where they can use your training? This is no place for you."

"It is until I do what I came back to do."

"What the hell does that mean?"

"You know what it means."

I met his glare with one of my own. "I won't stand for guns. And I won't put up with threats, either. I'm fed up with yours."

I stepped into the room and shut the door behind me. "I'll make you a deal, Ted. Leave now and I'll give you a letter that will keep you in your uncle's good graces. I gather that's how you've been making it so far."

Silence.

"Let's get to the basics. You know damned well if Uncle Oliver were to pull the plug, you'd be a financial paraplegic."

Even that didn't appear to make any mental ripples in that mocking, half-smiling, flint-eyed face.

"Look, Ted. He asked you to go back to Philadelphia. Surely, he has something in mind for you. Take him up on it. Picos is due here tomorrow. Probably his last trip before the rains get too heavy, the river gets too high. Go back to Oriximiná with him. Get a boat from there to Santarém then fly on to Belém. Three flights out of there to Miami every week."

He began to rub the gun's short barrel with an oily cloth.

I shook my head in frustration. "Listen to me, damn it. If you've blown whatever money Oliver sent you in the hospital, I can advance enough from the Station's cash fund to get you to Bélem. You can call him from there."

All that got me was a tight little grin. "My little adventure with Felicia was only a passing incident in your miserable existence, Turkey. What you've done to me is permanent. You think I'm going out of here like nothing happened?"

"Throw the damned gun away." Or else? What else? My problem was I didn't have a viable "else." I swung around, yanked open the door and stomped out.

***

"More coffee?" I asked.

"Gracias, but no." Capitán Picos flashed his startlingly white teeth in a quick smile. "No time for another." He set down his empty mug. "Lucky to be here today. The weather, it breaks. I load fast. Hard going against the current, but I know you need the gasoline."

"I really appreciate your getting up here with that." I nodded toward his two crewmen, my two Bororos and the half dozen G-string-clad Indians who had appeared from their village to help Jheem and Haree. With manpower alone, they wrestled the last of the bulky gasoline drums up the bank and rolled them toward the storage shed.

"Tomorrow could be too late for the trip up here, señor. A bad storm last night upriver. A flood up there. In Tiago. I hear a man—a doctor, they say—was washed away in his car. And all that water heads this way. Tomorrow the current will be big. Even today it was a fight to get up here." He grinned. "But we make up time going back. Maybe a speed record going downstream."

I stood. Last chance, but just maybe… "Hold up a few minutes, amigo. I may have a passenger for you." I trotted to the residence. Banged on Ted's door.

This time, he opened it only a crack. "What the hell, Turkey?"

"Get your gear together. The steam launch is here. You can ride it back to Oriximiná right now."

"You gotta be kidding. I'm here until I decide not to be. Tell the spic he's leaving without me."

I glared at him. "The who?"

"Your fat Mex with the Humphrey Bogart launch. Did he come to get me?"

I tried to swallow my flash of anger. "No doubt you noticed all those gas barrels Picos brought in. Fuel for the generator."

"Gas barrels?"

"What in hell were you doing while all that was going on?"

"Taking a nap."

"A nap. Christ. Well, you've turned down your chance to get out of here easily, Teddy. We won't be seeing him again for quite a while."

"I got business here, Turkey."

"You got nothing here. You should go with Picos."

"I'll go when I'm ready to go, Turkey." He slammed the door in my face.

I walked back to the mess shack, fuming. Picos gave me a quizzical look.

"He's staying here," I said. "Sorry." Sorry wasn't even close. I was boiling.

Picos stood and I walked with him to the riverbank. He thrust out a chunky hand. "Adiós!" And down the bank, he scrambled, only an eighteen-foot slope now, I judged. His crewmen were already aboard.

The outdated launch grumbled into life. One of the crew cast off the retaining lines. Picos gave me a farewell wave, and the launch labored into the current, sliding sideways until it straightened southward for the long but swift downriver run back to Oriximiná.

***

Next day, the waning afternoon's overcast shrouded the compound in eerie half-light.

The saturated forest floor squished under my shoes as I trudged to the mess hut after a long stint in the lab. A few days ago, I'd culled six candiru from their large holding tank and put them in a smaller one with barely two inches of water. Purpose? To determine how long they would survive in stagnant, unoxygenated water. For shipping purposes. Yesterday, they were alive, but barely. I estimated another day would kill them all. And it did. I opened my notebook. Did I really have to be so meticulous in my note taking? I knew I was using the lab as an escape.

A flutter of distant lightning reminded me of Picos's reporting the flood in that unfortunate town upstream...what had he called it? Tiago. Floodwater up there had nowhere to go but down the already swollen Trombetas.

I was disgusted with myself. I had missed a golden opportunity to hamstring Ted Rebner. I was no gun expert, but way after the fact, I realized that every one of the parts I had seen on the floor at Ted's feet had to be a necessary component of the pistol. If I'd had the smarts – and the nerve – to feign interest, kneel, study the parts, divert his attention and snatch just one of them, that damned gun would be inoperative. Opportunity lost.

What would have been his reaction? A part misplaced? Panicky search of the floor. Not under the cot. Not behind his travel bag. But that damned Durkin knelt here.

So what could he have done about the blank stare I would have given him?

But I'd done nothing. Blown the opportunity.

In the mess hut's humid warmth, Ted was already seated at the table. He didn't so much as nod when I walked in. Felicia, in white blouse and slacks and carrying her yellow rain slicker over her arm, arrived as I sat down.

"This awful, sticky weather. I hate it!" She hung the slicker on one of the nails near the door. "How are you feeling, Ted? You seemed so depressed this morning." Apparently, she still hoped to penetrate his emotional wall.

"How else can I feel in this frigging mud hole?"

"You had your chance to get out of here," I fumed.

"I told you, I have..."

"Yeah, yeah, I know. You have 'unfinished business' here."

Dinner was Agata's necessarily limited menu of broiled white fish with lemon sauce, an entrée that obviously didn't please Ted at all. I disregarded his grumbling as we passed the platter around the table. I'd had it up to here with the man's griping about the food despite Agata's efforts to vary our basic fish diet.

The conversational dead-end persisted until a crash of thunder jolted the building. Rain began to pelt the mess hut roof.

"Jesus," Ted muttered. "I'm so damned tired of all this."

"And I'm so damned tired of you!" I lashed out.

He grinned. "I see I hit your mad button."

I clamped my teeth against burgeoning fury. "I might be able to make arrangements by radio with that seaplane pilot," I said in desperation. "Get you out of here before the rainy season gets fully underway. You could be on your way in a day or two."

"Nice try," Ted said sourly. "I am not going anywhere until I…"

"This is delicious," Felicia interrupted. "We're so lucky to have Agata. Honestly, she can make almost anything palatable."

Ted turned toward the stove and sniffed. "Fried bananas again? Jesus." He pushed out of his chair. "All yours," he said to no one in particular and stomped out into the downpour.

We watched him make his uneven way toward the residence.

"Maybe you're overestimating Ted's attitude toward you, Emmett," Felicia suggested. "I realize he keeps muttering about some kind of vague plan he's got…"

"He's got more than that. He's got that damned gun. We're isolated with a seriously unstable man." Agata, stacking dishes at the sink, glanced at me. "All of us," I added.

I finished my banana dessert. Then realized I'd forgotten to record the output of the Electrophorus. "I have to go back to the lab, Felicia. I'll be over to the residence in a couple of minutes." I headed out into the murk.

With a wooden prod, I agitated the big eel, read the voltmeter, then pulled my notebook from the work-counter drawer. The familiar routine failed to calm me. The unremitting lightning flares and rolling thunder struck me as a portent of onrushing disaster over which I had no control.

17

The generator cut out for the night. Our dangling 60-watt bulb faded to black. I lay on my cot. The only sound was Felicia's gentle breathing. She had dropped off before the light went out, but I stared in the darkness at the invisible ceiling. I was a scientist, a lab man suited to impersonal research. How in hell did I deal with a mental case, the arrogant nephew of my employer? Ted outweighed me by a good fifty pounds. A dumb, revenge-bent bastard, now armed with a Colt .45. What should I do about the gun? About him? What could I do?

I hated myself for my inaction. But what choices did I have? Maybe, with the help of the Bororos, rush him with a club? Hope he'd go down? Tie him up? Then what? Call Capitão Rolha? Or somehow force Ted to agree to have the rescue plane take him off our hands. With the river more hazardous every day, would either Rolha or the Norseman pilot even chance a trip up here?

The cot creaked under my twitching. Impossible to get comfortable. Couldn't sleep. Ted with the damned gun pointed right at me. Felicia screaming… I hallucinated. So damned tired. Couldn't sleep…

***

What woke me at sunrise was the undeniable menace in Picos's warning. The heavy rain upriver was surging this way. I had a plateful, all right. No way out after my stupid loss of the Whaler. The dangerously rising Trombetas. A scramble-brained dolt armed with a pistol.

I envied Felicia's steady, quiet breathing. Lucky woman. She could sleep late, dress leisurely, amble to the mess hut for her customary orange juice, slice of canned brown bread and coffee. Then wander the compound. Immerse herself in fiction from her stack of paperbacks. Work on the tropical flower sketches she had recently begun. While I... Hell, while I faced the fact I didn't know how to handle Station Four's apparently inescapable slide from uncertainty to trauma. Or worse.

God, how I would welcome a return to those few incredible weeks when Agata and I had been the Station's only residents. Those days of sweet...

At first light, I pushed off the cot and dressed. I needed to keep a close eye on the damned Trombetas. As I neared the riverbank, I could see out there in the powerful current more tree limbs drifting fast, racing chunks of broken construction wood, even a big bloated...what? Looked like an unfortunate tapir drowned in the upstream flood.

Across the river, the rising sun had been swallowed by a thick overcast. But at the moment, no rain in this depressing gray morning. From the bank's crest, I glanced down. The river had risen another...

My God! Spread-eagled face-down on what looked like a faded blue wooden door wedged against the dock lay a man in black slacks, white shirt. A small man, about my size.

"Hey down there!"" I called. "You okay?"

No response, but I thought I saw his head move.

I scrambled down the weedy slope, less than a fifteen-foot challenge now. Crouched on the dock to peer at this astonishing flotsam. Saw a rise and fall of his narrow back. Heard him groan.

I reached down, gently prodded his shoulder. Another groan. I grabbed the cold bony wrists. His fingers were locked around the door's edge. One by one, I pried them loose. With a mighty tug, I slid him headfirst off his door, up the four-inch difference between door and dock, and laid him out on the splintery boards.

He mumbled something I couldn't decipher. Hoping he had no internal complications, I rolled him over on his back, yanked out my handkerchief. Dipped it in the river. Mopped his pasty white forehead. His eyes fluttered open. Squinty, iron gray eyes. Ginger hair cropped short by careless scissors. A couple days' beard, gray-flecked. Late forties, I guessed.

"Glad to see you're alive. Can you sit up?

"Maybe," he gasped, "with a little help."

I slipped an arm under his shoulders and got him into a slumpy-shouldered sit. He coughed up a mouthful of water. Spit it on the dock.

"Better," he mumbled.

"Take a few minutes."

"What a...ride. I'm lucky to be alive."

"We need some help to get you up the bank. You okay to hang on down here a few more minutes?"

I was back in five with Jheem and Haree.

"These gents are on my staff. You doing okay?"

He forced a smile. Wide-spaced little teeth in a narrow, pointy-chinned face. "I'm not ready to run a four-minute mile, but I think I'll live."

"How about standing?" I grabbed his arm, but he made it mostly on his own, breathing heavily through his mouth.

"Rough trip," he managed. "You an American?"

"I nodded. "You, too, I'd guess."

"Yeah. Name's...John..." He coughed. John...somebody cleared his throat. "Balti...Baltimore."

"Emmett Durkin. I'm chief of this place."

"What place?"

"The Rebner Foundation's Marine Research Station Four." I peered at him "Let's get you up the bank." I motioned to the Bororos. They each took John by an elbow.

I pushed his door away from the dock and it swirled off in the current. With Jheem and Haree's help, wobbly-legged John made it up the steep slope. At the crest, I asked, "You need some dry clothes. I have some spare..."

"I mostly dried off lying down there. Still a bit damp in the front, but I'm okay."

"I guess you can use some breakfast."

"Coffee for sure."

***

As Agata poured coffee for our visitor, Felicia joined us. Ted stomped in behind her.

Both of them stared at our bedraggled drop-in.

"My wife, Felicia," I said. "And Ted Rebner. Our surprise guest is 'John,' I think you said. But I didn't catch your last name."

"Yes, John. John...St. John." Raising his mug with both hands, he took a long drag. Set it down. Glanced at us. "The Reverend John St. John."

I needed help with an armed loony and God sent me a minister?

Felicia stared at him, perplexed. "How in the world did you get here, Father?"

"I plucked him off a door the current had pushed into our dock," I told her.

"A door! But how on earth...?

"Let the Reverend eat his breakfast, Felicia. Then maybe he will..."

"Where was your ministry, Father?"

"Upriver. Sixty, seventy miles." He drained his mug. "Might I have a bit more of this excellent brew?" Agata poured anew. "God bless you," St. John said with a benign smile.

"What's up there?" Ted blurted.

"Up where?"

"Sixty, seventy miles upriver, you said."

"Oh. Tiny village. Hit hard yesterday by the flood."

"What denomination are you, Father?" Felicia wondered.

St. John paused mid-sip. "Eh? What denomination? I'm a... an Episcopalian."

"You were the village priest, Father?"

"Ah." He waved a hand and gave Felicia a benevolent smile. "No need to call me 'Father.' I'm not Catholic. Yes, I did have my parish there. For just a few months. Making fine progress, too. Excellent progress among the heathens. Then came the deluge. Washed me straight into the river, and the Lord provided my means to survive. God bless the Lord. Might there also be a bit more of that bacon?"

As Agata reached over his shoulder to replenish the bacon platter, I saw his eyes focus on her emerald. In reflex, her free hand moved protectively to the pendant.

"Tell me," St. John said as he wrenched his gaze back to me, "what precisely do you do here, Emmett?"

I was impressed he remembered my name through the strain of getting him up here. "Research on the toxicity of certain marine fauna. Basic calculations of the voltage output of my Electrophorus..."

"He runs a goddam...sorry, Reverend." Ted sounded oddly contrite in the presence of this cleric. "It's a real chamber of horrors over in that lab. You won't believe what he's got in there."

"I'm surprised you even remember what is in there, Ted." I didn't look up from the slice of canned brown bread I was spreading with strawberry jam, one of my favorite jungle treats.

"What did you say is your parent organization?" St. John asked. "You mentioned it down on the dock, but I'm afraid it's slipped my mind."

"The Rebner Foundation in Philadelphia. It funds biological research in dangerous fauna. There's another Station in Chad, one in the Palau Islands, a third in the Australian Outback. We're Station Four."

"And the money comes from...?" St. John persisted.

"Private donations and government grants." Peculiar question from a man of the cloth, I thought.

He took another bite of boiled egg. "How long have you been here, Emmett?"

"About a year and a half. This is our second rainy season."

"Supplies come from...?

"Up the Amazon from Belém, the nearest big city. Then to Oriximiná to be relayed here by steam launch."

"Perhaps I could arrange passage on that launch."

I took a drag of coffee. "I'm afraid the launch just made what is probably its last trip until the rains subside."

St. John turned to Felicia. "Do you enjoy it here, Mrs. Durkin?"

"Not in the rainy season, Reverend."

He offered her a glowing smile and pushed back from the table. "Well, gentlemen and good lady, apparently until transportation is available, I seem to be unavoidably obliged to you."

"You can bunk with Ted," I told him. Intriguing combination. A sinner threatening to compound his transgressions and an Episcopal minister. "There's an extra cot in the supply shed."

"I'll give you a hand," Felicia offered.

I rose hurriedly. "No, I'll do it." I held open the screen door for our displaced parson. Our pace across the compound was more of an amble, with St. John apparently near physical exhaustion. Yet he managed to stay remarkably alert as I played tour guide.

"That's the lab building back there between the mess hut and the riverbank. Residence over that way. The long, tin-roofed building we're heading for houses generator at one end, our radio link to civilization in the other. Supplies in the middle."

When we reached it, I unlocked and swung open the center door. We stepped in and I rummaged about for the cot. I caught his quick visual inventory of our cases of canned edibles, various emergency items, crates with arcane — surely to him — scientific supply items. For a fellow who had spent God knew how many hours buffeting downriver on a tippy door, he seemed very perceptive.

"Here it is." From a stack of plastic-protected bedding, I tugged a tightly strapped roll of canvas and wooden components. "If you can manage that bundle of sheets and blankets, I'll tote this."

He shouldered the bedding, and we walked to Ted's end of the residence, surely not a site of appealing ambience to our mannerly guest. Ted was no housekeeper. A rumpled blanket humped on his cot beneath the bunched mosquito netting. Ratty-looking trousers draped the back of the room's only chair. A dirty shirt sprawled on the small table. Discarded socks dotted the planking around the luggage lumped beneath Ted's cot. The room of a college freshman finally out from under Mom's stringent thumb.

"Sorry about..."

"This will do fine," St. John said graciously.

I lowered the cot kit to the floor. "The mosquito net and its framing are with it. The frame bolts together. Sorry about the primitive arrangements, Reverend. We're not set up for comfort."

"This is ample, Emmett. Ample. Oh, there is one thing. Where's the cr...the bathroom facility?"

"It's the little shed back there at the edge of the forest. I'll have Agata bring you a washbasin. The water pump's just outside."

"Outside," he muttered. Then he brightened. "Sorry. I should be thanking the Lord I'm alive." He said that with a peculiar little smile. Not at all becoming to a man of the cloth.

I walked back toward the lab more in reflex than by design, my attention still on St. John. There was something about this man, I realized, that made me uneasy. Maybe because after dutiful church going with my parents, I kept my beliefs but didn't need them reinforced every Sunday. Now here was a cleric, all graciousness. Could I be feeling a touch of guilt?

Or was I put off by his ingratiating smoothness? Why did I have the feeling he was laughing at us as he laid on his Godly chatter?

18

Our Reverend failed to appear for lunch. No surprise, in view of his downriver jaunt. Ted hobbled in, of course. I wondered what he and St. John talked about, if they'd talked at all. Felicia greeted our more imposing "guest" with a quick smile but got no response. Agata bustled around the table, her expression blank. The three of us ate in uneasy silence until Ted blurted, "Sixteen today."

His damned push-ups. "That's great," I muttered. But I couldn't avoid wondering, again, what his goal was, and what he thought he would do when he reached it. Lunch turned out to be a study in silence that wasn't broken until Ted crumpled his paper napkin, tossed it on the table, stood and, without another word, clumped toward his room. I had the uneasy feeling he and St. John might find some common ground that Station Four could well do without.

"Well, that was charming," Felicia said, eying Ted's uneven gait. "Me for temporary escape to my sketch pad."

I walked into the fetid mugginess with her. As I turned toward the lab, she grabbed my hand. "Do you have to go to the lab, Emmett?" she asked softly. "Might you consider a...siesta? Like we used to, back before I..." Her voice trailed off.

This was a surprise. "Now, I always go back to the lab after lunch, Felicia. You know that." Lord, I thought too late, how stuffy can I be?

She gave me a wicked little smile. "Never an exception?"

"Unfortunately, I'm in the middle of evaluating the spawning potential of the..."

She laughed. "Oh, for heaven's sake, Emmett. Call me if you want me."

Odd, I thought. She never worked in the lab. My mind was already on the Gulf puffers. Their spawning potential, I decided, was zero.

Discouraged by their uninteresting aquarium environment, by captivity itself, or some other damned thing. I made a notebook entry of the negative outcome, completed the rest of my regular afternoon observations and added them to my pages and pages of handwritten notes. Then I stared into the afternoon's dismal drizzle. And wondered: Did the Foundation really care?

***

With St. John's appearance, supper became almost burlesquely formal. Or were we all uncertain how to react to our rejuvenated guest minister?

"Bless you, my daughter," he commended to Agata as she offered him the platter of baked river catfish. The Bororos had delivered again. Line caught or netted? Either way, not easy fishing in the strong current. When we all had been served, St. John cleared his throat.

"I'm afraid I have been remiss in my calling. Perhaps you will chalk that up to a bit of disorientation from my uncomfortable ride down the river. But now, if we could all join hands?"

What? Even Ted looked nonplussed as we all held hands. I felt ridiculous, but as we walked across the compound, I had whispered to Felicia, "Play along until we can figure out this guy's game." She was complying nicely. As was I. Ted was the last to link our little circle, obviously wondering what the hell this was about.

St. John bowed his head. "Bless this food," he said solemnly, "and to us, thy services."

Felicia gave me a raised eyebrow. As St. John looked up, Agata leaned over my shoulder to place the coffee pot on the table. His eyes darted to her dangling pendant, stayed there for a long moment. That, I did not find comforting.

"I trust you've settled in at the residence?" I said by way of diversion.

"My refuge from whatever may next befall. Can't complain. Dry quarters. Palatable sustenance. A compatible companion." He nodded at Ted, who was busily working on his baked fish.

"Um, yeah," Ted managed.

Ted compatible? Had to be a Station Four first. I found that more than bemusing. I found it disturbing.

***

A creak. I woke to impenetrable darkness. And a vibration. My mosquito net was being pulled aside. I felt weight on the edge of my cot. For a muzzy-headed moment, I thought Agata had stolen in while Felicia lay asleep not ten feet away.

"Emmett?" Felicia's whisper. Why a whisper? "Are you awake?"

"I am now."

"Shh, shh. I don't want them to hear."

"Who?" I pushed myself up on my elbows. "Hear what?"

"Please, Emmett. Keep your voice down. You know the wall between this room and theirs is thin as cardboard."

I couldn't see her, and I was confused — not only from being awakened by an invisible weight on my cot, but also by her unexpected closeness.

"It's our friendly minister."

"St. John? What about him?"

"I've been thinking and thinking about him. Can't sleep."

"What about him?" I asked her again.

"Emmett, he's a fake."

If there's anything I don't need, I thought, it's another complication. "Based on what?"

"Please! Keep your voice down." I heard her take a deep breath. "Well, he told us he's an Episcopal minister."

"That he did."

"But when I called him 'Father' he didn't like it."

"I'm sorry, Felicia, but my Congregationalist upbringing doesn't give me a clue to what you're talking about."

"It didn't hit me until I remembered Chrissy."

"Who's Chrissy?"

"Christine Gladwyn, from Wilmington. She was my first-year roommate at The Hastings School. An Episcopalian."

I shifted my weight to my right side. I needed sleep, but what she was saying started my wheels turning. "What about Chrissy?"

"She and I used to have long gabfests about religion. My parents are ardent Presbyterians, but I wasn't much of anything once I went away to prep school."

"Felicia…"

"I remember being surprised when she told me Episcopal ministers are called priests. And Chrissy told me they encourage their parishioners to call them 'Father.' Don't you see?"

Was she onto something? I felt I had seriously underestimated my wife's acuity. Not for the first time, either. When she suggested I learn the Bororos' names and call them by name, I thought that was unnecessary. But when I finally did it, their demeanor had brightened from that of sullen servants to the far more helpful attitude of eager assistants.

"Emmett?"

"Huh? Oh, yes, I do see." Why would St. John object to being called 'Father' if he's an Episcopal priest? "That's really observant of you, Felicia."

"I don't think he's a minister at all."

"Based on one seeming inconsistency? That's not exactly solid evidence he's not what he says he is. What's been bothering me is not whether he is a reverend. What sets me on edge is his attitude. Sort of, I don't know, laughing behind our backs."

"Yes, and I've noticed more than that one 'inconsistency,' Emmett. Not only the 'don't call me Father' business. There's the way he said grace. That's a pretty universal one he butchered. And what minister or priest of any denomination would say 'God bless the Lord'?"

"He said that?" How had I missed such an inane redundancy? But do a couple of slips make the perhaps still-disoriented man a fake? "Is it possible he's no more than a quirky cleric?" I asked her. "He's been courteous and cooperative. I don't know what his game would be...if he has one other than just getting back to civilization." I realized I was trying to talk myself out of the growing uneasiness I felt about this guy.

"Don't all those odd little slips worry you?"

"I guess I was more concerned with the rapport that seemed to be coming about between him and Ted. Now, you've got me really wondering about our holy man."

To my surprise, I felt her gently caress my cheek. And with that little intimacy, I suddenly felt a closeness to her I'd thought I would never feel again.

Then she slipped beneath my rumpled sheet. "At least I've got you seriously concerned about our peregrinating pastor."

"At least. And if he's a fake, you've also got me wondering why he calls himself an Episcopalian."

She snuggled close. I began to stroke her back gently. "Picked it out of the blue," she suggested. "Or maybe when I called him 'Father,' he assumed we were Catholics, so he came up with a denomination he mistakenly thinks is far from Catholic. Not as safe ground as he thought. He set himself a trap."

"As good a guess as any," I murmured.

Her fingers trailed down my chest. "What do we do about him, Emmett?"

"We have Agata hide her pendant."

"Oh, you noticed that, too."

"St. John—or whatever his name is—can't keep his eyes off it."

"And then?"

"We keep playing along, Felicia. Eyes wide open."

"I wonder about Ted, too. I mean, him and St. John together. Do you think Ted knows he could be a fake?"

"God knows. Maybe it takes one to know one."

"Oh, hell, Emmett," she sighed, and her fingers turned gently mischievous. "Let's worry about all that tomorrow."

"Felicia, you're taking my mind off..."

"That's the idea," she whispered." She struggled out of her pajama bottom. "Never easy in a cot," she said with a little chuckle. "No, lie still, my dear, and let me work my womanly wiles."

***

Much later, she kissed me tenderly then stepped back to her side of the room. I heard her cot creak as she rearranged the netting then lay down. In minutes, her quiet breathing in easy sleep was the room's only sound.

I stared into the blackness, mind aglow. I hadn't expected such erotic intimacy with her ever again, especially at her initiative. For the first time since she returned from the ignominy of her Belém defection, I knew I still loved this woman of surprises. And I knew whatever unpredictable fate we faced here, we would face it together.

In the forest behind the residence, I heard a squeal, a sharp little cry of terror.

Some prowling animal had become prey itself. A diversion, but my thoughts snapped right back to St. John. Why pose at all? Is St. — whatever his name might be — actually something he doesn't want us to know about? Why would he put on a phony act for us? Why pass himself off as a minister? Ah, got it. What occupation receives universal respect and trust? That of a man of the cloth.

Still, how much of a threat was the man? When I checked him on the dock for broken bones, I would have found a concealed knife or gun. So he was no threat that way... I caught my breath. I put him in with Ted, and Ted had that damned gun.

So if St. John actually was some sort of charlatan, or even a thief, what could cause him to pose a problem here, I wondered? Agata's and my salaries were deposited in escrow by the Foundation. Funds for the Station's supplies were handled by the Foundation's local rep in Oriximiná. I did have the pay for the Bororos in the cash box here in the residence. The cash box. Ted knew about the cash box. Could that be enough to tempt an overconfident petty crook?

Then I felt a little chill. Agata's emerald. The reverend couldn't keep his eyes off it.

I rolled over on my back for my contemplative stare into the roof trusses, invisible in the blackness. A petty crook? Was St. John on the run? Did we have a fugitive in our midst? Or was our guest addled by his wild downriver ride and, despite all his slips, exactly who he said he was?

Sleep did not come easily.

19

"**S**o gratifying to be among friends," St. John pronounced at breakfast. "You have no idea what I've been through. My poor flock up north must feel forsaken by their pastor—through no fault of my own, of course." He gestured toward Ted. "Pass me that delicious brown bread, would you?"

I had to restrain myself from laughing in his face. What should I call his attitude? Pious mockery? I was sure he was playing with us ignorant common folks, enjoying his deception hugely.

"The bread? Sure thing, Reverend." Ted slid over the stack of canned brown bread slices. At Station Four, fresh bread was out of the question.

Through the rest of the meal, I kept a close eye on these two. I sensed a growing compatibility between them. That, I was convinced, was not good. St. John's close-set squinty eyes and his scraggly untrimmed beard did not look remotely clerical.

After breakfast, with St. John's cloying gentility failing to override my uneasiness, I lingered in the mess hut. As Felicia, Ted and St. John had left, Agata caught my eye. Gave me a little nod toward the kitchen area where she now waited.

"What is it, Agata?" The comfortable aromas of bacon and coffee contrasted with her obvious concern. She peered around me for reassurance we were alone. "That man."

"St. John?"

"Sim. He is no man of God."

"How can you know that?"

"My school was a Catholic mission. I know priests. How they truly are."

"Agata, he says he's not a priest but a minister. Not a Catholic."

"No matter. I feel it." She touched her breast. "Aqui. Be careful with him. I... care for you," she whispered.

My throat tightened. "Thank you, Agata," I managed. "Obrigado."

I turned to leave then turned back. "I see you are not wearing your pendant. I hope it is in a safe place."

She nodded. "Senhor St. John also noticed."

"You are very observant, Agata."

"Observador, sim. Por favor, you be also, mi querido."

Felicia pointed out St. John's religious inconsistencies. Now Agata questioned his unparsonly aura. Both my perceptive women had warned me. I left the mess hut and slogged across the compound. At the residence door, I stomped the mud from my shoes, kicked them off and stepped in.

Felicia looked up from a needlepoint kit she had brought back from Belém. "What was that all about? Your little confab with Agata."

"Voices down, Felicia." I nodded at the partition. "Fact is, she's as leery of St. John as we are."

"How in the world would she see through him?"

"Mission schooling. Apparently gave her a sense of how a member of the clergy would behave. That, plus who-knows-what arcane instincts came with her mixed heritage?"

I stripped off my slicker. "I'm certain he's a fraud, but I can't figure out what he's up to."

Seated on the edge of her cot in cream slacks and a white shirt, she looked like a vulnerable child. "He's playing with us."

"Why? It's got to be more than that."

She put the needlework aside. "If he's hiding who and what he really is, he's got to be on the run from somebody or something."

"I could use the radio to have Picos check with the Pará police. Maybe they..."

I stopped.

"Emmett?"

"On second thought, I'm not too eager to check with Pará."

"Why not?" She peered at me. "What's wrong, Emmett?"

"While you were...away, a Pará police captain arrived to check on Ted's fall down the bank. And he took special notice of Agata."

"Agata?"

"Said she met the description of a Manaus woman his department was on the lookout for. I stood up for her, and he left. Apparently, he accepted my assurance Ted's fall was an accident, but I suspect he was not entirely convinced Agata isn't the woman he was looking for."

"Agata is from Manaus, Emmett. What do we really know about her?"

I hesitated.

"Emmett?"

She deserved to know. "Agata told me she did have serious trouble in Manaus, Felicia. She stabbed her husband."

"My God, Emmett!"

"He beat her, Felicia. But he was an employee of the polícia, so she ran. I think she could have made a good case for self-defense, if she had found a lawyer up there with the guts to go up against the police. But she knows Manaus a lot better than I do."

"So if what's-his-name…"

"Rolha. Capitão Rolha."

"If he was so suspicious of her, why didn't he take her in? Didn't he at least question her?

"Rolha knew the date she had left Manaus. He asked me when we hired her. I told him a date that gave her an alibi."

"You lied for her?"

"Her husband was a wife-beater, Felicia. Rolha told me that. She'd suffered injuries."

"He beat her?"

"A lot."

"This…Rolha told you that?'

"Agata told me that. We had a talk after he left."

And a whole lot more. The memory of Agata's bronze nakedness, her dark tipped breasts, her shadowed triangle of black curls shot a flash of heat through me. I looked at the floor.

"Oh," Felicia said.

Rather speculatively, I thought, with her eyes still on me. I met her aqua stare. "I suspect the husband got exactly what he deserved."

Her pupils, pinpoints of perception, drilled into me. Then, her voice unexpectedly soft, she said, "Everything here has become so upsetting. I keep thinking back to how we were before…well, before we came here. She smiled impishly. "Remember when we…?"

"You mean when I was working for Mote Marine?"

"Before that."

"Our clash of trays that began our…"

"No, after that. When we first…"

"I sat beside her on the cot. "Oh. In the canoe we rented at Lake Okeechobee. From Captain Rogen, I think his name was."

"Drogen. Captain Drogen," she said. "Then off we paddled, amazed at how big the lake was. Like paddling on the ocean."

"All those secluded bays."

"The lily pads. Miles of lily pads."

"And Captain Drogen's comment. Remember that? 'If you fall overboard, just stand up.'"

She giggled. "That whole huge lake wasn't more than four or five feet deep."

"We watched the sunset." I still remembered all this so vividly.

"And the moonrise. And you began to..."

"I was inspired. Then I was afraid to go any further."

"And I was afraid you wouldn't." She gave my thigh a playful squeeze. "Then you did."

"And you didn't stop me."

"I encouraged you, Emmett. I was so eager."

"And I was so clumsy. An American oddity. A virgin at twenty-three."

She gave me a little grin. "I've never told you, Emmett. It was my first time, too."

"It was?"

"I didn't want you to think I was such a frump that nobody ever wanted me. Then you came along. I was so excited, I was ready to do anything to please you."

"A frump and a nerd," I said with a chuckle and took her hand. "Rub them together, and you get..."

"Fire! I glowed. That first time—in a canoe, of all places—is my absolute favorite memory."

"Yes, you really did glow. My God, what are we doing in this place, Felicia? We should have stayed in Florida. I should be working on my doctorate."

Wishful thinking. I knew damned well what I really should be doing. Facing Ted and somehow getting that gun away from him. Sending St. John on his way. But how? In the Station's fragile canoe? I wasn't facing either of those situations, because I couldn't figure out how.

I slipped my arm around her shoulders. "This place is killing us all." It blossomed Felicia then corrupted her bloom. Propelled me into Agata's embrace. Brought us an indolent, useless Ted Rebner, then brought him back venomous. Gave us St. John and whatever questionable intent had arrived with him.

"How in hell am I supposed to deal with all this?" I muttered.

"You are the Station Chief," she said.

I stood, then bent down and kissed her. "That's the irony. I've got to get to the lab."

I walked across the compound on leaden legs, slumped on my stool and, without enthusiasm, opened my notebook. But the station's research work seemed far less urgent than its problems.

"Ted tells me..."

My head jerked up. St. John stood in the doorway, a smile crinkling his ferret face.

"Startled you? Sorry. I'm told you have a fascinating collection of marine life in here."

"Ted is correct."

St. John walked in unbidden, bent down and tapped a fingernail on the glass of a tank no one else had ever taken an interest in.

"Ugly little devils. Look like flat worms."

"They're tremadota. Fresh water flukes. Their eggs are parasitic on marine snails. When the larvae are released from the snail, they seek a warm-blooded host. Such as..." I realized St. John had nudged me straight into lecture mode.

"Such as?" My uninvited visitor prompted with a smile that bared his picket fence teeth.

"Such as human. People wading in their bare feet, for example. At the least, the larvae can cause severe skin infections. At the worst, fatal schistosomiasis."

"What in the world is that?"

"An infection that can gradually destroy the internal organs."

"Sounds decidedly unattractive." He moved down the left-side row of tanks.

I went back to my notes, unable now to concentrate. Maybe try a little probing of my own?

"Your parish," I said. "Where was it?"

"I told you, Emmett. Washed away by the rising river."

"Capitán Picos, the owner of our steam-launch service, told us he'd heard a man up in Tiago had been washed into the river up there."

St. John straightened from his tank study. "That must have been me."

"A doctor, Picos said." Gotcha, Reverend.

Silence from St. John. Then he brightened. "A doctor? Oh, of course. A doctor of divinity. You see? Myself, undoubtedly."

Undoubtedly. "And before that?" I pressed. "Back in the States, I assume."

"Oh. Uh, in Western Maryland. A small parish near my hometown of Lonaconing, about twelve miles from Cumberland."

When I plucked him off his door, I thought he had said Baltimore. "Big congregation?" I asked.

"Not big enough. "That's why I took up missionary work."

As an interrogator, I realized, I was not exactly Perry Mason's eclipse. If St. John was a liar, he was a good one.

"How about you, Emmett? What's your background?"

"High school in Peoria, my hometown." That with reluctance. I couldn't ignore the creepy feeling he was storing every detail. A smiling fraud. Felicia had alerted me. Agata had convinced me.

"Then the University of Chicago," I went on without enthusiasm. "Master's in marine biology at the University of Florida. Research in Sarasota until I was tapped for this job."

I kept that brief but still had the crawly feeling anything I told St. John could be too much. I made a try at question reversal of my own.

"You went to school in Lona...what was that place?"

St. John gave me a tolerant smile. "Lonaconing, Maryland. I was born there, went to school there."

"Lonaconing has a seminary?"

"A what?"

"A seminary. Where did you train for the priesthood?"

And St. John stumbled again. "The...ah, the... But I told you I'm not a Catholic."

Ah, Felicia, you should hear this. "I assume Episcopalians train as well as Catholics," I persisted. "Where did you attend?"

"Baltimore." Had he remembered his blurt down on the dock? "What are these little beasties, Emmett?" He pointed at the lemon yellow frogs in a nearby aquarium.

"Poison-dart frogs." I was tiring of this verbal cat-and-mousery. "I really must complete these notes, St. John."

"Call me John. Please. My apologies for the interruption, Emmett." St. John walked out smiling.

Five minutes later, he was back, his smile still in place. "Did you check the river level this morning, Emmett?"

I sighed. "Of course I checked it. I check it every morning."

"How far below the top of the bank was it?"

"About ten feet, same as yesterday."

The smile vanished. "It's less than that now."

Less than ten feet clearance left? I'd hoped the river had crested and would miraculously begin to recede. Was St. John using an imagined rise in river level as an excuse to come back here and continue pumping me? Or could the man be right?

"I'll take another look." I set my notebook and pen aside and followed him out the lab door. Our Reverend, or whatever he was, had become an aggravating itch.

Fine rain filtered through the leaf canopy. Its filmy veils shrouded the river in mist so dense I couldn't make out the far shore. The Trombetas appeared to be a fast-flowing sea, stretching eastward into infinity.

I stood beside St. John on the lip of the bank and felt a twitch in my belly. The man was right. The level had risen. The water's edge had climbed past the anchor stakes.

As if they had materialized out of the mist-laden air, Jheem and Haree stood beside me. At first glance, I was startled by what appeared to be their huge erections.

So was St. John. "What in the world are those for?"

Then I remembered why the near-naked Bororos wore those phallic hand-woven sheaths. "To protect them from penetration by the little candiru catfish that periodically infest the river," I told him. "They'll burrow into any body opening."

He gave me an odd look. "Guess I was lucky."

"Lucky you had pants on."

Without a word from me, slim Jheem and pudgy Haree plunged down the bank and waded waist-deep to the downstream stake. They worked it loose, untied the slack line from its dock cleat then carried the iron rod and its line up the bank and over the lip. With a sledgehammer Jheem had left at the crest, he pounded the rod deep into the ground behind the bank's rim a few feet past the up-current rod. Haree ran the line down to the upstream side of the floating dock and secured it. Then they shifted the existing upstream line and rod into place as the new downstream line. The whole elaborate process resulted in the anchor rods now firmly on more solid land behind the bank's edge. Through the process, the dock had bumped just a few feet down-current but still hugged the bank.

"Impressive routine," St. John said. "The Indians live here? I haven't seen any such lodging."

"They walk in daily from their village a mile or so upriver." Now he knew the extent of Station Four's little garrison.

As I eyed the new stake locations, my anxiety notched upward again. Last rainy season, my and Felicia's first, the river's rise had never required placement of the dock's anchor stakes behind the lip of the bank.

St. John caught my expression. "Not good, is it? If the river comes up another few feet, what then?"

"Fortunately the station's topography slopes upward from here. Not a lot, but I've estimated the river level would have to rise several feet above the bank to flood us out entirely."

"Not a pretty thought," St. John muttered, gazing into the encroaching water. Then with seemingly renewed energy, he faced me. "We must put our trust in the Lord."

"Could be." You want to play man of God, try this, you fake. "Perhaps you would honor us with a brief prayer service, Father."

"Please, not 'Father,'" St. John protested. "A prayer service? I believe each in his or her own way can be just as effective as a formal service. And unfortunately, my prayer book washed away in the deluge that brought me here."

Very slick, Reverend. I gave him a benign smile of my own. "Then silent prayer will have to suffice."

"Indeed. If you will excuse me, I do relish the opportunity to meditate." St. John offered me a stiff little bow and strode back into the compound.

I stared at the river. If it climbed over the bank, the lab and residence would be first to flood. Station Four's obvious low-budget construction plan had not included elevating the buildings on pilings. Flooding the compound by more than a few inches would threaten the residence, lab and mess hut. The generator-supply-radio building would probably survive unless the flooding reached a depth of several feet.

I wasn't certain of the land's exact elevation beyond the Station's west boundary, obscured as it was by the forest's heavy understory. If the ground continued to rise back there, and if the upriver cloudbursts were to persist, there was no way to predict the ultimate depth of flooding across the compound. Even were we to find temporary refuge on dry land back there in the understory, the compound would be unlivable. If the radio flooded out, we would be marooned, living with the hope Picos might suspect what had happened.

Or would he have his hands full coping with a flooded Oriximiná?

I turned away from the sliding, mud-stained water. Its rise might well be our ultimate problem, I realized. But my immediate concerns were Ted the Unpredictable and our gap-toothed liar who called himself the Reverend St. John.

At supper, the four of us sat glumly listening to the spatter of rain on the mess hut roof. Agata bustled about the table, serving thick slices of fried boar. I almost wished it were fish again to prompt Ted's familiar gripe. Even that would be a welcome break in the oppressive silence.

He obliged anyway: "Tell them about your trip down the river, John," he said through a mouthful of wild pig. In his tone more than his words, I sensed a growing rapport between these two.

Felicia caught my eye. Same reaction?

St. John put down his fork, leaned back and gazed at the exposed roof framing. "A traumatic experience indeed."

I waited for him to add, "My children," but he passed up the opportunity.

"Late in the day up there in my scattered parish, I was rushing to comfort a parishioner on the other side of the stream that cuts through the village. The road crossed it, not by a bridge but by a shallow ford. I didn't realize the rain had washed away the ford…and then some. The old Chevy I had borrowed didn't make it across."

He paused, sipped his coffee. Put it down. "Do you know that just a couple of feet of water is enough to float a car? I found that out the hard way. So downstream we floated. For a minute or two. Then the car began to sink. Couldn't open the door against the water pressure. I barely had time to scramble out the window. The car went under and so did I. When I came back up, something whacked me on the shoulder. A door. Wrenched off its hinges by the flood. The good Lord had intervened."

He paused and glanced around the table. "I rode that floating miracle down the flooded creek then into the river."

"The Trombetas," Felicia said, leaning forward in apparent rapt attention.

"Exactly. The Trombetas. For a long pull. I have no idea how long I was on that God-sent door. Hours and hours. Through rain squalls, then burning sun, then rain again. I passed out but still managed to keep my grip on the edges of that blessed door. Then I remember a thud and silence. When I came out of it, I was up on your dock. And there was Emmett, kind soul Emmett, patting my brow with a cool cloth."

Kind soul Emmett didn't doubt this guy's story. In fact, I thought it could be the only honest words I'd heard from him since he drifted in. But nothing he'd said had lessened my suspicion that we had in our midst an opportunist at best. And at worst? Only God—and maybe by now, Ted—knew.

"What a horrible experience," Felicia said. "How lucky you are, Reverend."

I liked her continued "Reverend" address. Playing along in the hope we would finally learn what pious John was really up to.

Through St. John's downriver story, I kept my eyes on Ted. And he kept his eyes on St. John. I remembered telling Felicia I felt Ted was a case of inertia—a real threat, but one needing a prod to spring him into action. I glanced at St. John. And was met by his speculative gaze. Then he shrugged.

"So much for horror stories," he said. He smiled at Agata. "Might I have a refill?" His eyes dropped to her breast line. The smile flickered. He had just noticed she was no longer wearing her pendant.

20

Another night of near sleeplessness. The Station was the bull's-eye of a flashing, crashing thunderstorm. Ear-numbing claps shook the residence. Rattled the walls. The walls? Oh. The rattling came from Felicia's archery equipment, hung as our only wall decoration then long forgotten.

The flashes through our lone window, the roll and bang of thunder, weren't all that kept me awake. The Station was slipping more and more into the hands of our two unwelcome "guests." Ted's return in itself was alarming. But I hoped, without real conviction, he would continue to find satisfaction in taunting me with threats, picturing himself an avenger but unable to take action on his own. I was concerned about St. John, our smiling, obsequious liar. Could he be the catalyst that would — when it suited his purpose — push Ted beyond his campaign of menace?

And what in hell could I do about it? They had the gun. And if there were no gun? Should I have Picos contact the Para Polícia? Even were Rolha to chance dodging river debris for a trip up here, what then?

"You tell me Senhor Rebner is making threats, Senhor Durkin? I am to arrest two men merely for what you say are threats?"

In truth, I had no real evidence St. John had anything in mind other than amusing himself in his ministerial role. Probably he was the washed-away doctor Pecos had mentioned. But a "doctor of divinity," St. John had corrected. Slick and quick, Reverend.

Picos. Our faithful steam launch skipper...and occasional collector of gossip. By now, might he have heard further concerning that storm-borne "doctor"? Something of use, or at least some information that might give me background on St. John other than what he himself had... manufactured? With that fragile comfort, I finally slept. Fitfully.

The sun and I came up at the same time; the sun out of the murky eastern shore rain forest; I out of a sleep haunted by the certainty of some approaching crunch point with these two schemers. And hating my uncertainty about how to face it.

I shoved the mosquito netting aside and peered through our little window. Light in the mess hut. Ever dependable, Agata already had the coffee perking. I pulled on shirt and slacks. Took a quick trip to the latrine shed out back. Brushed my teeth at the water pump out there. Padded back through the residence. Felicia lay in a fetal curve. Defensive as she slept?

I walked out to the riverbank. For a change, the water level had stabilized some feet below the crest. The sun broke through. A bright moment in a gray morning. I strode on to the mess hut. To my relief, Ted and St. John were late risers this morning.

"Bom dia, Agata." That from my meager stock of Portuguese.

She smiled. "Good morning—" she glanced across the compound—"mi querido."

I saw her eyes shift to the west end of the residence. She shook her head. Slightly but significantly. Then turned back to me.

"Puffer fish for dinner?" she asked. Only half joking, I suspected. "For two?" Or maybe not joking at all.

"Tempting, Agata. But no."

"But then...que?"

"I'm not sure what. I hope to find out more about the...Reverend."

"Nossos imposter."

I nodded. "Sim." Without much appetite, I downed a couple of hot cakes, a mug of coffee, pushed back from the table. "I'll be up in the radio room, Agata. No need to tell the others."

The post-sunrise air had thickened to clammy dampness. I slogged to the west end of the compound, the turf yielding under my shoes. No activity in the residence. Fine with me. The less Ted and St. John knew of my actions this morning, the better. I opened the door at the storage building's north end, shut it quietly behind me. Settled down in front of the radio and flipped it on. Picked up the mike.

"Station Four, Station Four calling Capitán Picos. Come in, Capitán."

Nothing. I tried again. And again nothing. Either he was out of his warped board shack, or maybe was out like a light from last night's whatever.

I tried a third time. Still no response. Waited a few more minutes, tried one more time. Again, nada.

Frustrated beyond good sense, I reached for the switch. Later, damn it. I wasn't going to give up on this.

"Picos aqui, Señor Durkin. Why you call so early?" There was life down in Oriximiná, after all.

"Sorry, Capitán. Muchas gracias for your response." With my Mexican friend, a touch of Spanish never hurt. "You remember you told me of a doctor washed away in the flood up north?"

"Ah, si. In Tiago."

"Have you learned anything more about him, Capitán?"

"Nada, nada. But wait. People from there have come here into Oriximiná. I will talk with them, si?"

"I think he has washed up here, and we are hosts to a con man."

"Con man, señor?"

"Thief, Capitán. Find out what you can about this Tiago doctor."

"He is there with you?"

"That is what I suspect. If you do hear anything more about the doctor, I will appreciate it mucho."

"Increíble! I will like to play policía secreta."

"Not secret police, my friend. Play detective."

"Ah, si. That is the word."

"Call me if you find out anything more. And gracias."

"Da nada, Señor Durkin. I like the game."

I closed down the transceiver. Slim hope. But maybe, with flood refugees straggling into Oriximiná, this was my only hope of prying into the recent activities of our "doctor of divinity." My short-range radio could reach only Oriximiná. Were it capable of contacting Santarém, though, would I have risked contacting Capitão Rolha?

On my way to the lab, I passed the mess hut. By now Ted and St. John—and Felicia—were engrossed in conversation. I kept walking. Without my presence, perhaps Ted and the Reverend might be tempted to impress a lady with some bragging that might be revealing. I pushed into the lab, disturbed that my concern about Ted and St. John was making the lab work my secondary interest. Now, I thought, I was clinging to my slim hope that "Policía Secreta" Picos might help me determine just who exactly was St. John and what in hell he wanted.

But the morning crept along with only silence from Oriximiná. Agata arrived with my mid-morning coffee, swept the place and left, throwing me a quick smile over her shoulder. A bittersweet reminder of far warmer moments past.

Lunch was another tense half hour. Routine now. An occasional "Bless you" from St. John for Felicia's passing the canned bread or Agata's refilling his water glass. Otherwise, silence. Meal times did not relieve my crawly feeling of impending calamity.

The afternoon dragged on. I had to reread each listless notation I entered in my notebook. Survival rates, specimen shipment notations, aquarium temperature readings.... My mind was elsewhere. Supper with St. John's increasingly superior attitude was no relief.

As we made ready for bed, I asked Felicia, "You learn anything useful at breakfast with Ted and St. John?"

"I'm not sure, Emmett." She kept her voice low, as I had. "Maybe a sense they have some plan, but they seem to be waiting for…I don't know what." She stripped off her panties and pulled on her pajama bottoms. "Did you get through to Picos?"

"I radioed Picos. I think he might pick up some info from Tiago flood refugees straggling into Oriximiná. He said he'd ask around about the 'doctor' he'd heard was washed away in his car." I pulled off my shirt. "So far, though, nada."

She buttoned her pajama top then ran her fingers through her caramel hair. "You know what I miss most out here in the wilds? Hairdressers. My hair's gotten so long."

"I like it long. I love it long." I touched her shoulder then took her in my arms. Held her. "Whatever happens, Felicia, I want you to know I love you, girl."

She kissed me fiercely. "That goes both ways, darling. It goes both ways."

In the fuzzy mental twilight just before sleep, I heard her say, "At breakfast, Ted did ask me where you were."

"What did you tell him?"

"I said I didn't know. And he said, 'I thought I saw him walking up to the supply shed.' Something like that. I think he was fishing."

"Why would he care where I was going?"

"Doesn't he know the radio is up there?"

"Yes, he does." And in an early fit of hospitality, I had told St. John about it, too. I pulled the sheet up to my neck and faced another near-sleepless night.

***

I rushed through my breakfast alone — hot cakes and coffee again — but not at all disappointed that Ted and St. John apparently felt no urgency to join me. Felicia walked in as I was about to leave.

And then: "Good morning, all!" A cheery greeting from St. John, entering behind her. By himself, for a change.

As if he read my mind, he said, "Ted's sleeping in for a bit this morning. Hope you won't mind."

Mind? I was relieved not to have to put up with the man's surliness. I shoved back my chair.

"You're leaving so soon, Emmett?" St. John asked. "I just got here."

He cared? "I have work to do in the lab."

He chuckled. "You always have work to do in the lab. What is the urgency, Emmett? We are obviously cut off from the rest of the world for awhile. Relax and enjoy the isolation."

Enjoy the isolation. What was this? "I'm afraid I'm a stuffy man of routine, Reverend. A scientific plodder."

"Well, stop plodding for a few minutes. Have another coffee. Be sociable." He sat back as Agata refilled our coffee mugs. "Thank you, my dear." He stabbed a fork into the hot cake stack and put three on his plate. Took a bite. "Delicious. My compliments, Agata."

"Obrigado, nossos ministro." She was playing along, too.

"Tell me, Emmett, what is the purpose of all this?"

"All this?"

"Station Four."

"The study of dangerous marine life. I thought I told you."

"I mean, the ultimate purpose."

This was so unlike the St. John I'd gotten to know and suspect, I wondered what was going on. "The ultimate purpose? To supply the Foundation with specimens of venom and such."

St. John smiled patiently. "I mean the Foundation's ultimate purpose." He threw a quick glance into the compound.

"I have no idea what the Foundation does with what I ship up there." Damned if I'd tell him what I thought they might be doing with it, but I saw no need to tell this guy. Why his sudden interest? Was he some sort of plant—a spy for a rival of the Foundation? Or for the Foundation itself? Dropped off just beyond the river's north bend to drift in here on his damned door?

Ridiculous speculation, Emmett. Get a grip.

I caught him flicking another glance outside. I turned slightly and flicked a glance of my own. Saw the residence's west front door open.

"Ah," St. John said. "Here comes Ted now." As Ted hobbled across the compound, St. John appeared to have lost further interest in probing the Foundation's mission. The conversation lapsed into weather banalities.

Then it hit me. St. John had been stalling my leaving for the lab. Until Ted appeared. Why, I had no idea.

I stood. "Time to get to work." And I walked to the lab...

Where I found the little red bulb near the corner of the work table, the signal that Picos had made an attempt at radio contact, lifeless. Bleak as the sunless morning. I slumped on my lab stool. Stared into the compound. Let my mind drift back to those glorious weeks when Agata would appear with two mugs on the mid-morning coffee tray.

The mornings we would sit here together, concerned only with our growing warmth for each other. That incredible first night we...

I shook my head. Not fair to Felicia now. Fair enough then, maybe. So apt a retribution for a wife I was convinced had coldly walked out on me. If she had given me only a hint she intended to come back, I wouldn't for a moment even have thought of anything more personal with Agata. Of course not. But in my anger and desolation at Felicia's apparent desertion,

I had behaved like a...I sighed. Rationalization of carnal behavior with the help. But it had been glorious. She still made my heart race.

I was in love with two women, but I knew I could live that love with only the one I had sworn before God to love.

I forced myself to haul my notebook from the work-table drawer. Sighed. Opened it... And the little signal bulb flashed bright red.

I shoved the notebook aside, switched off the signal's circuit and hurried out of the lab into the sullen morning. Picos had to have heard something. Or was he calling to tell me he hadn't? I walked past the now busy mess hut, feeling all eyes on me. Caught a smug smile on Ted's doltish face. At the north end of the long supply shed, I stepped into the radio room. Shut the door. Switched on the transceiver. Picked up the mike.

"Station Four, Capitán Picos. Come in.

Nothing.

"Station Four, Capitán Picos. Come in, come in."

Still nothing. Truly nothing. No click of his keying his mike. No static. No background noise whatever. Like listening to a vacuum.

Yet the little red bulb indicated a signal had come through, and Picos always stayed on the air for at least ten minutes to give me time to get up here. Had he broken contact for some reason? Never happened before.

I frowned at the transceiver. Had something become disconnected in there? Rusted out in this corrosive climate? Or maybe a tube had worked loose. I was no radioman, but at least I could take a look.

I pulled open the top drawer of a nearby cabinet and pawed through the clutter. Found a screwdriver. Back to the transceiver. Pulled the power cord out of the wall socket, upended the thing—and found out what I should have already checked. Phillips head screws.

Back to the tool drawer, traded the blade screwdriver for one to fit the cross-cut screw heads. The six retaining screws in the housing were corroded but surprisingly easy to turn. The access plate came off, but I couldn't get the guts of the thing out until I pulled off the on-off-volume and tuning knobs and removed the four little screws holding the speaker to the housing. Sweating now, I finally slid the works out where I could check them. I felt like the ignorant driver of a stalled car lifting the hood and staring at the innards without the remotest idea of what all that stuff was.

One big surprise. There were no loose tubes. There were no tubes at all. The last time I saw the inner workings of a radio was during my grade-school days. Electronics had marched on without much notice from me. I fingered a printed circuitboard replete with a welter of little multi-colored thingies. I wiggled them gently. All seemed neatly soldered in place. The only wires were the incoming powerline connection and a thin little wire from the circuitry to the base of the three-inch diameter speaker.

I tested the powerline connection. No give there. Gently nudged the speaker wire. And it came loose in my fingers. I bent closer. A half-inch of copper wire remained soldered to the speaker contact. I skinned back the insulation of the wire in my hand. No gleam of copper until I worked the insulation back almost an inch. I squinted at the ends of the stub on the speaker and the wire in my hand. Looked as if there had been nice, clean cuts — with a half-inch of wire missing. Then the empty end of the rubbery plastic insulation tube had been neatly threaded back on the stub. Though it had looked normal, the wire had a gap. No sound from the speaker. Damned clever.

And no wonder the corroded chassis screws turned easily. Now I knew why St. John was stalling me at breakfast. Ted must have left the residence by their room's back door, skulked along the understory back there to the rear of the storage building. Then slipped around its north end into the radio room. Only at that point — and when he came back out — would he be visible from the mess hut or lab. He must have gotten in here before I came out of the residence. Then I showed up, and St. John had to hold my attention until Ted stepped back out of the radio room, again briefly exposed until he sidled back behind the storage building then down to the residence, into their room through its rear door, then out the front door to breakfast. Clever, you bastards.

I had never felt a need for locked doors at Station Four. I should have left my small-town sense of riskless openness back in Peoria.

What now? I studied my disabled transceiver and pondered. The wiring to the speaker looked as if it had enough slack.... I carefully stripped away insulation to bare an inch of the copper wire. Working delicately with a pair of needle-nose pliers, I twisted the exposed wire to the stub on the speaker base. Two turns were all I dared. I reassembled the transceiver, tightened the casing screws, plugged in the power cord. Switched the thing on.

"Station Four, Station Four. Come in, Capitán."

And, to my relief, he did.

"A problemo, Señor Durkin? I answer your call, but you do not answer mine."

"A little technical mix-up, Capitán. Have you anything for me?"

"Si. I talk with four people from Tiago. Big, big flood up there. Wash out much of town."

"The doctor. What of him?"

"Ah, si. El médico. One niña from there knew a song he taught them. 'Big M, little c, big C.. u...r...e,' " he chanted with a laugh.

"McCure?" Jesus. Con-man cute.

"Si. Simon McCure. People with not mucho dinero go to him. Pay what they can. For medicina, he sends them to the farmacia, but no prescribe — how you say?"

"Prescriptions."

"Ah, si. No prescriptions."

Aspirin for aches...and appendicitis? Doctor of divinity, my eye. Dr. McQuack. Robbing the destitute.

"When the flood comes," Picos said, "he has in his office una hombre, muy colérico...angry. His wife is near death because of McCure. And McCure runs, jumps in his car. Drives off into the storm then into the creek. They never see him again. That is all I find out."

"Did they tell you what this McCure looked like? Tall, short, mustache?"

"They say he was not a tall man. Your size, señor, with a small barba... beard. Sorry I do not have more."

Suspicions confirmed. How much more did I need? Tiago's "McCure" had to be Station Four's "St. John."

"Most helpful, Capitán. Muchas gracias. Let's hope the weather gets no worse. Station Four out."

I trudged back to the lab. Warnowski had gone bonkers here. When Picos took him away, and Felicia and I walked in, the Station was empty. No one there. How in hell was Warnowski supposed to do it all by himself? In the long run, he hadn't. He went nuts. I didn't have his loneliness problem; I had plenty of company, including two bastards I could do without.

As I passed the mess hut, Ted called, "Trouble?"

And I didn't think he'd had talent for anything, let alone electronic sabotage.

"Radio's dead." I kept walking.

"Oh, really?" he said with a mocking smile. "No way to call for help now."

21

Another day of tension, though this morning dawned unusually benign. The sky clouded over but seemed at rest. A welcome rainy season lull. No lull, though, in the Station's social tensions. I felt they, like the weather, must soon burst.

At breakfast, Ted smugly exuded menace and St. John chirped his now sarcastic sounding, "Good morning, all." He and Ted disappeared, then four hours later: "Ah, the luncheon repast." Another hours-long fade-out, then: "Dinner hour at last." Through each meal, his constant, "Bless you, bless you," grated on me like sandpaper on sunburn.

By then, I'd had it. St. John's phony niceness made me decide to go ahead with something I'd mulled over for days – something no gentleman would even think of. But now I was ready to do whatever I could to protect my women – and myself.

In a fit of glee, one of my college roommates had told me about the technique. His delight in describing it turned me off. Then. Not now. Tonight if sleaze might serve, so be it. With dinner over, Felicia returned to our residence room. Then Ted hobbled off to his. But apparently afflicted with an urge for small talk, St. John stayed put.

"Tell me, Emmett, how long do you plan to stay in this soggy wilderness?" In the generator's soft yellow output, his spaced teeth glittered.

"My contract's up in five months."

"And then?"

"Then? I don't know." I needed him to leave.

He settled back in his creaky camp chair. "I wonder what my life would be like if I'd had a scientific specialty like yours. Seeing the world at Foundation expense."

"Some world, this." For Pete's sake, Reverend, get out of here.

"It's surely different from — where did you say? Peoria?"

I nodded.

"Well, it looks like Ted and I are stuck here with you, Emmett. Marooned in the jungle until the launch can get up here." He sat back, laced his fingers over his flat belly.

Not in the least distraught, he looked like what he was, a schemer with plans falling neatly in place.

If he insisted in staying here to jabber, this could be the time to make an offer I'd been mulling over the past several days. An offer that could be worth a shot, though it would truly maroon the rest of us if the compound flooded. I gave him what I hoped was a constructive glance. And I said, "There is the canoe."

He laughed. A reaction I hadn't expected. Leaned forward to plant his elbows on the table. Supported his pointy bearded chin on woven fingers. Bemused attention, I thought. And mocking body language. "If your steam-launch captain is afraid to venture up here in that debris-cluttered river," he said with an indulgent smile, "what chance would the canoe have?"

"Picos would be pushing upstream with the debris coming downstream toward him. You would be moving downstream, along with the flow of whatever comes down the river. And at the same pace." I leaned toward him. "Look, St. John, I'll be glad to have you and Ted take the canoe. Tomorrow. You both can get out of here during this lull. Before the rainy season's peak hits."

Our eyes locked. I hoped to hell he would take this "easy" way out.

He sat back. Tented his fingers. Broke his stare at me to contemplate the ceiling. "A generous offer, Emmett. And for river cruising, a canoe surely beats a door." Then he gazed at me again for a long moment. "Were I to take you up on that offer, what would you and the women do?"

As if he gave a damn. Or did he think we might know of some other less risky way out of here?

"Take our chances," I said with a shrug. "Hell, St. John, I can't leave here. I've got a contract." I wasn't about to tell him that based on the failure of last season's rise to top the bank, I expected the Trombetas to repeat that nail-chewing but ultimately benign performance this year. Even were it to flood into the compound, a night in the storage building at the Station's higher west end should see us through the worst of it. Concern about the weather was worrisome but not even close to my growing apprehension at what this confident con man and his now-cohort Ted could be hatching.

"You are willing to give us the canoe and you will 'take your chances'? How self-sacrificing of you, Emmett. I'm impressed. Such benevolent concern."

"Love your neighbor, St. John."

"Do unto others, Emmett."

I stole a glance at Agata stowing the last of the supper dishes in the cupboard over the sink. She met my look with eloquently raised eyebrows.

"In this difficult situation, I'm trying to do what I can for our guests, Reverend." I can lay it on, too, Big M, little c, big C, u-r-e. I wondered if the distraught husband who chased him out of Tiago might have straggled into Oriximiná. Pictured him riding upriver asnarl on Picos's launch. Slim hope, that. More likely, were our bogus Reverend to canoe into that little burg, I relished the idea of that same agitated guy throwing the phony doctor-cleric back into the fast-flowing Trombetas.

Come on, St. John, get the hell out of here.

And with that thought—mine—he stood, stretched. "It has been pleasant talking with you, Emmett," he said with an undertone of disdain. "I wish you a good evening. You, as well, Agata," he called.

"Boa noite." Pause. "Reverend." Her tone was pleasant enough, but her eyes bored into me as St. John sauntered into the hazy twilight. I waited until he reached the residence and closed the door behind him. Then I told Agata, "I need a glass."

"Áqua? Should I make more coffee?"

"No, just an empty glass. The biggest one we have."

Puzzled but ever-responsive, she reached deep into the cupboard, rummaged a bit then withdrew a tumbler.

I shook my head. "Too heavy. Let me have a look." I pawed through the assorted glassware and found one big as the tumbler but thinner. I stuffed it in my pocket. She gave me a perplexed look but said nothing. I turned to leave and felt her fingers on my arm.

"El ministro," she said with disdain, "he is impatiente, mi querido. Be careful. Muito careful."

"I must do what I can, Agata. You, too, be careful of these men—both of them, especially St. John. I don't like the way he kept looking at your emerald pendant. And his face when he noticed you no longer wear it." I thought a moment. "It might be a good idea to let me hold it for you until they're gone."

She shook her head. "I thank you, mi querdo. But I think it best if I... if I hide it myself."

I was stunned to see her eyes mist. My God, can she be thinking St. John would be coming after me along with Ted when they failed to get the emerald from her?

"Hide it well then, Agata. Boa noite." With the glass in my pocket, I walked across the compound with purpose.

Felicia, curled up on her cot in blue-striped pajamas, set aside her paperback novel. "What in the world were you and St. John talking about, Emmett? I thought you were going to spend the night in the mess hut."

"I offered him the canoe." Mindful of the thin dividing wall, I kept my voice down, as had she.

"The canoe? But the current. And that stuff floating out there."

"He and Ted could probably make it down the river. They'd be moving along with whatever junk is ramming downstream. I think they'd have a better than even chance of reaching Oriximiná, even Obidos. I won't care whether they make it or not. Once they leave the dock they'll be out of our hair. There's no way they can paddle back against that current."

I sat beside her and pulled the glass out of my pocket.

"What's that for, Emmett?"

"I'm going to try a little trick I heard about in college."

"With an empty glass?"

"One of my roommates told me about it. Driving back to Chicago after a weekend at home, he stopped overnight at a motel. Just as he was getting into bed, he heard some—well, intriguing sounds in the neighboring room. He took a glass from the bathroom, held it to the intervening wall. And listened."

"Why the glass?"

"It amplifies the sound coming through a wall. If it works, let's see if we can hear whatever conversation my canoe offer may stir up." I felt myself being pulled into something...well, sordid. But by now, St. John's deception and Ted's continuing threats were just too damned much. I was about to toss civility out the window.

Felicia touched my elbow. Uh oh, here comes a morality lecture. But she said, "So what did he hear?"

"Who?"

"Your roommate with the glass."

"Oh. Big disappointment. He finally realized the purrs and moans in the next room were a TV porn movie. But the point is...the glass did pick up the sounds. That's what I'm hoping..."

From the other side of the thin partition, I heard the mutter of voices. Like every night. I looked at Felicia. Her eyes were alive with anticipation. The barefaced snoopiness of what I was about to try didn't bother her. Why should I let it trouble me? I stood, gently applied the rim of the glass to the plywood partition. Glued my ear to the glass's bottom.

All I could make out was a low rumble. Ted. Then a higher pitched mumble. Our Reverend. I caught Felicia's expectant stare and shrugged.

"Seems this juvenile experiment is a flop," I whispered. "Guess I need FBI-strength electronic bugs and a receiver." I wondered about my roommate's report. Purrs and moans? Or just another dorm myth? I put my ear back on the glass for one last try.

"...tired of waiting." Those words suddenly morphed out of St. John's high-pitched mutter. He must have wandered closer to the wall.

"...gotta do what I gotta do." A rumbling profundity from Ted. Apparently they were moving around in some agitation.

"...do it, for Christ's sake. We gotta get out while the weather..." St. John.

"...every night, damn it. I'm tired of your..." Ted.

"...offered me the canoe." St. John. Then laughter from both.

"Offered! ...take what the hell we want when we want." Ted.

"Yeah, but when?" St. John.

"Just before...big one hits. I do...thing. We're outta here." Ted.

"Your thing? You don't...guts to..." St. John.

"You grab...I'll take care of him. Then...canoe." Ted.

"...you had the guts, we'd already..." St. John.

"You'll see...just before...next big storm. 'Reverend.'" Again both laughed.

"It fools them...not an inkling." St. John.

"Praise the Lord!" Together, with high hilarity.

End of conversation. I put down the glass.

"Anything?" Felicia asked.

I sat on her cot and took her hand. "Mostly confirmation. I could hear only snatches of what they were saying when they moved near the wall. The Reverend is no reverend, of course. That's a big joke between them. He's a con man, that's for sure. And a thief—or about to be. I heard Ted tell him, 'take what we want.' Looks to me like St. John-whatever-his name is waiting for Ted."

"To do what?"

"To do 'what I gotta do,' as Ted put it."

"All those awful threats to 'get even,' Emmett." She shuddered. "What are we going to do?"

I put my arm around her shoulders and pulled her close. "I'm damned sure going to come up with something. It sounded as if St. John gave Ted a deadline."

"Deadline?"

Bad word choice. "Well, a limit on how long they will sop up our hospitality before..."

"Before what, Emmett?"

"Before getting me out of their way then looting the place. I gathered they're planning to have Ted do his 'thing,' loot the place, then grab the canoe and get out of here just before the next big storm hits."

"You're really scaring me, Emmett. Do you really think Ted would... would actually..."

"You've heard all his damned threatening. He's just plain nuts, Felicia. Who knows what he'll do? And he's got that damned gun."

"What is there here to loot?"

"Agata's emerald, obviously. And Ted knows about the cash box in here. He's seen me paying Jheem and Haree. My guess is our bogus parson is after the cash box, a bonus, along with the emerald. There's no big fortune in there, but up in Tiago, he was using his talents to take what had to be small payments from his 'patients.' A potential cash haul of reals worth a few hundred bucks may have him salivating."

"We can hide the cash box somewhere, Emmett."

"Even if it's pilfered, no big deal. What really gets to me is that they would have the gall to steal anything at all."

We sat in uneasy silence. Just a few feet from two bastards deficient in conscience but long on self-indulgence, I thought. Picket-toothed, ever-smiling St. John, a travesty of the clerical role he was enjoying; Teddy the Unready, trying to work up the guts to take his damned "revenge" so St. John could get on with his pillage of Station Four. Three threats: St. John. Ted. And that goddam gun.

I pulled her close. She was trembling. I kissed her gently then more reassuringly, I hoped.

"Oh, God, Emmett," she whispered. "You know what Ted's planning to do. How can you be so calm?"

"That's not quite how I'd put it, Felicia. My guts are in a knot. I'm trying like hell to come up with some...some plan."

"Plan?"

"They're convinced we've been taken in by St. John's act. Both of them are sure we're going to sit here in amazement while Ted does what he thinks he's going to do to me; then they grab and go."

"Emmett, I'm frightened to death."

"I've got ice in my stomach, too. I've never been personally threatened like this. But, damn it, Felicia, I'm tired of playing along with these two. At the moment, they're swaggering around in a rush of overconfidence. I've got to make a move. And m'dear, I'll need your help. It's a gamble, but, by God, we're going to shake them up."

22

I stood up from the breakfast table, slapped my shirt pocket. "Damn! I forgot to bring that new Bic pen for the lab."

"You must have left it in the residence, dear. I'll bring it over to you after I've..."

"No. I'll get it, Felicia. Finish your breakfast."

As I pushed out of the mess hut, I heard her ask Ted, "I've been wondering. When you were at Cornell, did you by any chance know Terry Wharton?"

"I'll leave you two to your Philadelphia memories," St. John said.

"No, Reverend. I want to ask you about..." Her voice faded as I strode off into the compound. Neatly done, Felicia. As we planned. Now hold those two in the mess hut and we'll see if my little scheme puts an end to Ted's nutso thoughts of revenge.

I walked through the unusually placid, almost bright morning to the front door of our residence room. Sauntered in then rushed out the back door. Swung right, trotted to the back door of the other residence room. This time I appreciated the Station's lack of door locks. Now for my second unsavory effort to disrupt whatever Ted and St. John had in mind. First my glass "stethoscope." Now this.

The neatly made cot had to be St. John's. The wad of bedding on the other one almost wore a Ted label. He had jammed his travel bag under the cot. I dropped to my knees and rummaged through a jumble of musty clothing. Nothing resembling a... Hold on. I felt something with hard edges. Pulled out the box of gun-cleaning equipment. Then my fingers closed on a smaller box that rattled. It was nearly full of .45 caliber ammunition. Where the lead bullets joined the brass cartridge casings, they were ringed with a thread of greenish mold. But that hadn't affected Ted's slaughter of poor Indy.

I sorted through the mound of shirts and underwear on Ted's cot. Ran my hands over St. John's trim cot. Checked the overhead trusses. Scoured the flooring's perimeter.

What I didn't find in Ted's bag, or anywhere else in the room, was the damned gun.

So much for Felicia's and my grand plan to search and defang.

I heard footsteps squelching toward the residence. Too heavy to be Felicia's. I made a quick scan of the room. All appeared to be in order — or appropriate disorder on Ted's side. I barely made it to the rear door when the front door latch clicked.

Hell with it. This whole thing was beginning to make my blood boil. I turned around and watched Ted lumber in. When he saw me, he reared back.

"So where's the damned gun, Ted?"

"You little shit." He shook his head in disbelief. Then he laughed. A nasty, self-satisfied rattle. "I figured you might pull a search, Turkey. The Colt is secure, fully loaded and secure." He threw me a mocking grin. Your trouble is you still don't realize who's in charge here."

"You and your hotel management training?"

"No, me and Johnny St. John. When the time comes..."

"Look, Ted," I decided to make one more try, "we're having a lull in the weather. It won't last long, but it can be your last chance to get out of here without swimming. You and St. John. I already offered him the canoe. It's only eight miles to Oriximiná. You can do it today. Leave all this misery behind."

"Jesus Christ, Turkey! You gotta be kidding." He slapped his game hip. "Leave this misery behind? It goes everywhere I go. And you're damned well going to pay for it. Pay big." His eyes looked unfocussed. He waved an arm. "Get the hell out of here!"

"Advice you'd better take yourself!" I snapped back at him. I pushed past, slammed out the front door and stomped up to the storage shed. My heart thundered. That son of a bitch! Now I was going to do what I should have done days ago.

I tore open the door to the radio room. Plunked down at the transceiver. Flipped it on.

"Station Four. Come in, Picos."

Nothing but background hiss.

"Station Four calling Capitán Picos. Come in, Capitán."

Was he out on a charter in this benign weather break? Unlikely, considering its uncertainty. Not bad at this moment, but capable of raging the next.

Then I heard a click.

"Picos here, Station Four. Buenos dias. Problema?"

"I need you to relay a message to Capitão Rolha in Santarém."

"The Para Polícia?"

"Si, Capitán, the Para Police." Things were racing way past my control—if I'd had any control to begin with. Even if Rolha were to get another look at Agata, the situation called for outside help. "Tell him the false 'doctor' from Tiago is here at Station Four. He now calls himself a minister."

"You have McCure there?"

"We have McCure. Calling himself St. John. And the man you brought here, the man with the limp, has a gun and is threatening to use it. Tell that to Rolha also. You understand, Capitán?"

"Si. Si, Señor Durkin. I will call Rolha pronto. Pronto, Señor."

"Gracias, muchas gracias. Station Four out."

I shut down the radio and pondered. For about ten seconds. If I was going down, damn it, I'd go down fighting. I stepped to the tool cabinet, yanked open the top drawer. Pawed through the hardware. Pliers? No. Maybe a screwdriver? Ah. I came up with a sturdy claw hammer. No, I didn't intend to rush back to the residence and beat Ted's head in. But if he dared show up in the lab with that damned gun, I hoped I would be quick enough to shatter his wrist. Hell, his front teeth. Whatever part of him was in range.

I slid the hammer inside my slacks, hanging its claw over my belt. Stepped out of the radio room nodding at Jheem and Haree, who were clearing encroaching underbrush behind the storage building. Possible allies in this, I wondered? My communication with them was mostly sign language. They were loyal, but a .45 pistol versus two machetes? I visualized one-sided slaughter and walked on to the lab. I set the hammer on the workbench, plopped down on the stool, and tried to get my breathing under control.

In a few minutes, St. John emerged from the mess hut. I watched him cross the compound and enter the residence where I had left Ted fuming.

I could imagine the conversation:

"Caught the little bastard in here looking for my .45." Laughter.

"He couldn't find his own ass with an anatomical chart."

I was thoroughly steamed—and frustrated. For an ugly moment, I tried to blame my predicament on my parents. A school-teacher father who impressed me with the value of negotiation versus the consequences of confrontation. An even harder-nosed mother who directed that attitude toward my observing social graces. Both parental approaches to problems had been easy to emulate, especially considering my not-overwhelming stature. I'd met a few shorties who projected an attitude of hair-trigger aggression. Dismissed them as victims of the disparaged Napoleonic

Complex. Look what happened to Napoleon.... And look what was happening to me, blaming my frustration on my parents, for God's sake!

I eyed the hammer, conveniently in reach but perhaps ridiculous. Could I actually disarm crazy Ted with a claw hammer if I was fast enough? Hopeless maybe, but I felt I was doing something aggressively positive at last.

***

The ultimate intent of these two wolves in our sheep cote was pretty damned obvious. But our Reverend was cocksure he had us totally bamboozled. Would we gain anything now by continuing to play along with his game?

At lunchtime, in they strolled. Smug, superior. "Oh, bless this food," St. John pronounced as he sank into place.

"Amen," Ted grinned and nudged my shoulder with an elbow. "Where's the gun, Turkey? Where could it be?" He plopped down and said to no one in particular, "This little shit had the nerve to search my room."

Silence. Agata stepped to the table to serve what smelled agreeably like fried chicken. The only bright spot in the day, so far. The Bororos had delivered again.

"No privacy for an injured guest," St. John said with a mocking smile, "and a man of the cloth. The Lord will..."

That did it. "Oh, come off it, McCure." I snapped. "We're onto you." I watched his ruddy face blanch. Felicia sat frozen, fork halfway to her mouth. Agata, pausing behind St. John, looked delighted.

St. John peered at me with a little smirk. "Did you misspeak, Emmett?"

"No, Doctor, Reverend, and whatever other roles you've played. You can drop the act."

St. John's expression was one of a startled man trying to recover – and thinking fast. Ted gaped at me.

"'Big M, little c, Big C, u-r-e,'" I quoted. "Since the kids in Tiago sang that in English, I assume you taught them that yourself. Cute."

His forced smile fading, our phony minister said, "What else do you know?"

"Doctor of Divinity St. John...Doctor of over-the-counter medicine McCure. Why don't you get out of here while you can? You must have made some money off your aspirin clinic up in Tiago. Isn't that enough?"

"If you must know," he said, again wearing that irritating little half-smile, "my entire bankroll washed out of my shirt pocket while I rafted down this damned river on that door. At the moment, I am destitute."

"Can't be a new experience."

"Part of the game, Sherlock."

"Jesus. It's a game?"

"Winners and losers, Emmett. I like to be the winner."

A predator projecting a sugary aura to disguise his vacuum of conscience. "And those poor, sick peasants up there in Tiago?" I wondered.

He shrugged. "So you are aware of my Tiago idyll. What can you do about it, Emmett? You own the store, but we have the gun."

"Damn it, McCure..."

"It's actually McArt. Martin McArt."

"What can I do about it, whatever the hell your name is? I'm trying to save your sorry butts by telling you to take the damned canoe. You're in luck. A break in the storms. Oriximiná is only eight miles downriver. Shove off now, and you can make it there before the Para Policia get that far from Santarém."

His hands gripping the table edge, Ted leaned forward. "You gotta be kidding, Turkey." He frowned at McArt, as St. John now called himself. "You can't be taking this little prick seriously. I thought you wanted the emer..."

"Shut up, Ted. I'm thinking. You say you called the police, Turkey?"

Ted threw me a grin. "Like hell you did. The radio's dead. I took care of that."

"And I fixed it. My call to the police got through."

"You 'fixed' it, Marconi?" Ted giggled. "You think we'd fall for that? More coffee, Agata," he yelled over his shoulder.

In silence, Agata poured him another mug, her face hard bronze. Her eyes flicked to mine then to the steaming pot. I shook my head: No. McArt mistook that for frustration. But he had it right. I felt my moment of dominance ebbing away.

I tried again. "Yes or no, McArt? Maybe the cops have already launched, but it's a hundred miles from Santarém to Oriximiná. Only eight miles from here. You could be there before they even came by on their way here."

And with luck, one or more of the Tiago refugees might recognize McArt and alert the local constabulary.

"So I have the canoe," McArt said.

Ted banged the table with his fist. "And I have the gun. Hell, we'll take the damned canoe whenever we want. I say we go nowhere until I do what I came back here to do!"

Again, his damned threat. A coward under all this bluster, I suspected. If he truly intended to blow me away, why hadn't he already done it?

"Ah, the ever-threatening menace man." McArt chuckled. "Give me time to think, Theodore. Reel in that runaway temper. We all need to regroup a bit." He threw me a toothy smile. "Dinner at six as usual, Turkey. Don't be late."

He ushered Ted out and followed him closely, as if he were blocking any action from his overwrought partner.

I gave Felicia a sigh of futility. For a moment—only a moment—I'd had McArt rattled. I found satisfaction in that. But I knew I had made a mistake. Instead of cutting the ground from under McArt, I was forcing him and Ted to play their hand. And I wasn't at all sure how they would play it.

"Now what?" Felicia said. Her face was ashen. At that moment, we heard a prolonged rumble to the north.

I looked at her, glanced at Agata. Thunder rolled again. Trying to keep my voice steady, I said, "Our peaceful little lull is about to end."

23

Icouldn't sleep. Neither could Felicia. We lay in each other's arms, hoping for mutual comfort in shared apprehension. To the north, up in the Acarai and Tumucumaque Mountains, thunder's thump and roll persisted.

Had I made a terrible mistake? "I should have kept my mouth shut," I said. "Should have let McArt keep on thinking we were taken in by his St. John act. Never should have told them I radioed Picos to send for Rolha."

I felt her arms tighten around me. "They didn't believe you, Emmett." I felt her warm breath on my ear. "They're sure they've put the radio out of commission."

"Ted's sure. But I doubt McArt wants to wait around to see whether I actually did manage to get through to Picos. My big mouth may have forced him to have a try at getting out of here."

"But isn't that exactly what you want him to do?" she asked softly.

"What worries me is how he will go about doing it. I thought I made it easy by offering the canoe. All they have to do is get in it and shove off. Trouble is, McArt hasn't impressed me as a man at all concerned with conscience. What he is concerned with is grabbing whatever he can on his way out. And I don't think he's worrying about how he grabs it."

The distant thunder rolled on. She shuddered and I held her tighter. "I have such an awful feeling, Emmett," she whispered. "Like something terrible is about to happen."

I kissed her neck. "Worrying is my job. Everything's going to be all right."

I didn't believe a word of it.

"Love me!" she demanded. "Oh, Emmett, love me. Please! I feel like it's the only escape we have."

I kissed her again, this time less with compassion, more with fire. She sat up and began to tear off her pajamas with a desperation that startled me. I wondered: is she thinking this might be our last time?

***

I woke in darkness, gloriously naked, curled against her warm back and soft buttocks. I slipped an arm loose, reached for my wristwatch. The luminous dial said six o'clock. Six and still dark. Lying here pleasantly numbed by Felicia's female warmth, I hated to get up. And I felt a sense of guilt—guilt for inflicting this rainforest isolation on her. Guilt for bringing her—both of us—to this anticipated paradise now whirling out of control.

In pre-dawn darkness, I began to roll gently off the cot. Her hand reached for mine. I thought she had been asleep. She took my fingers in hers, gently urged my arm upwards, guided my hand between her breasts and closed her fingers over mine.

"Stay," she whispered. "Just like this. Stay."

Last night's desperate lust had ebbed into her need for comfort. "For a little while," I whispered.

In the face of what my racing brain told me was potential calamity, we lay comfortably together. I would remember this unexpectedly tender moment for the rest of my life. If there was to be any "rest of my life." We faced a weak-minded idiot, a warped misfit with a gun bent on "revenge." A stone-broke con man urging him to get on with it so they could loot and run. How could this be happening to my once secure little community?

Felicia's breathing calmed, became rhythmic and deep. Reluctantly, I eased my hand from her breasts. She murmured but didn't waken. I slipped off the cot and quietly dressed. Made my out-back morning visit. Latrine and pump. Low clouds hung over Station Four like a gray quilt still darkening the morning in eerie half-light. A fine mist dampened my face as I stepped back into the residence, smoothed the sheet over Felicia's shoulders then walked out our front door into the sodden compound. The mess hut's light glowed through the oppressive mist. Up in the northern mountains thunder still rolled. The constant rumbling sounded as I imagined distant artillery would sound. And just as ominous.

By the time I reached the mess hut, my shirt was damp. Despite the cloying heat, I felt a chill, a feeling of impending disaster I couldn't shake.

Agata appeared to be the Station's only other early riser.

"Bom dia, Senhor," she said formally. She peered toward the door, realized I was alone, and offered me a warm smile.

"Looks like I'm your first customer."

In her sexless smock, her lustrous ebony hair in a severe knot, she brought the coffee pot to the table, poured into one of the mugs already set. "No, mi querido." She tilted her head toward the west end of the residence. "They were already here."

"So early?"

"Sim. I had to dress first. They banged on the door, wanted coffee quick. Then they wanted sandwiches."

"Sandwiches?"

"Cheese and bacon. They took sandwiches with them back to room."

What in hell was going on with those two now? Every other morning, they had dawdled at our breakfast table like men with nothing to do, exactly what they were. Until now. I didn't like the sound of this. Not at all.

Or, on second thought, had they finally suspected I really had repaired the radio? Were worried my story of contacting Picos for the Para Polícia might not be a bluff? Realized they had no time to lose if they were to reach Oriximiná before Rolha got that far from Santarém? Well, good riddance!

Then my flash of exuberance faded. They could very well be planning that plus whatever else they had in mind before shoving off, all of it accelerated by the threatening turmoil to the north. That cannonade again vibrated the dark morning. I forced a couple swallows of coffee and jumped to my feet.

"Jheem came here, too," Agata blurted.

"Jheem? For breakfast?" I was joking. The Bororos always went straight to work His appearing at the mess hut was unusual.

"Not for breakfast." She frowned. "He say he and Haree stay in the village today. Too much rain north. He say they get ready for too much water."

That was ominous enough, but it didn't override her sandwich report.

I reached down for one more quick slug of coffee "Back in a few minutes, Agata." I rushed into the compound. The only sound came from the north; the very stillness of the air at Station Four in itself felt thick with foreboding. I hurried across to the residence, found Felicia already in her dark slacks pulling on a blue T-shirt.

"Come with me," I told her. "We're having breakfast together."

"Emmett, what…"

"Something's going on. Ted and McArt rushed through coffee then took sandwiches back to their room. I don't want you to be walking around alone."

She frowned, concerned with my obvious unease. "Why in the world would they do that?"

"I have no idea. But I don't like the sound of it at all."

She looked as concerned as I felt as she trotted back to the mess hut with me. Agata had laid out pancakes and bacon. We ate in silence; then I said, "You should stay with me in the lab." More reflex than good sense.

"On second thought, that might not be a good idea." If Ted was nuts enough to actually accost me in the lab, I wouldn't want her with me.

She toyed with her pancakes then pushed her plate away. "I'm sorry, Emmett. I just don't have..."

"I'll walk you back to the residence. Please stay there—with the door closed."

"There's no lock."

"I know, I know." I heard a thread of real concern in my voice and hoped she didn't notice.

She paused in the doorway. "But if St. John...if McArt is after the cash box, what should..."

"I'm thinking, Felicia." In a jumbled rush, I asked myself what in the hell should I do now? But I had no good answers. Have her stay here with Agata? But the emerald makes Agata a target, too. Buy our way out of this? Take the emerald and the cash from the box, hand them over and wish Ted and McArt bon voyage?

I felt my breakfast threaten to come back up.

"On balance," I finally said, "the residence may be the best answer. They have no business with you. Just say nothing. Let them take the cash. Only a few hundred bucks worth of Portuguese reals. Not worth getting hurt over." Or worse. "The Bororos can wait for their wages until the Foundation replaces it."

We stood in the mess hut doorway, still uncertain. I said to Agata, "The emerald is what McArt wants. Better let me hold it until they're out of here."

"There is no need, Senhor. He will not find it."

"Agata, it would be better if I..." Her expression told me I was not on the winning side of this. I began to sound like a man in panic, lurching one way then the other. Maybe all this was one big false alarm. Maybe after I stripped McArt in front of everybody, he couldn't face us again. Who knew what was in that shifty brain of his? And who knew what in hell Ted thought of doing with that gun of his—if he thought at all?

Was I overreacting? I hoped so. I hoped Ted was still the inept dodo I thought he was when he first showed up here.

I took Felicia's hand. "Come on, I'll walk you back to the residence. Then I'm going to the lab and try to figure out this mess."

Figure it out? I thought I had. More or less. If Ted was bent on some sort of personal revenge, at least in the lab it would be isolated from the women. So I told myself.

I opened the residence door for her. "Remember what I told you, Felicia. If McArt comes, just let him take the cash. Don't even try to get in his way."

"Emmett, do you really think..."

"I hope to hell I'm overreacting. Hope they'll just take the canoe and get out of here." I kissed her with more fervor than a simple see-ya peck. I tried to sound offhand, but I felt a rope of apprehension around my chest.

"Maybe I'm a victim of my own imagination."

"Oh, God, I hope so, Emmett."

"See you at lunch."

I headed for the lab.

***

I needed something constructive to do. A task that would refocus my jittery attention. Something to help me keep a grip on why I was here at all. I glanced at the rows of bubbling tanks, the big forty-gallon eel aquarium, the smaller tanks of ceaselessly circling puffers, the stingrays half-buried in their four inches of sand, the darting little candiru... I spotted the unexpectedly filthy Phyllobates terribilis tank. I owed my bright yellow poison-dart frogs a cleaner environment than that murk.

I readied a spare aquarium to hold the deadly little frogs while I scrubbed theirs.

Took a pair of latex gloves from the work-table drawer. The milky poison exuded from the poison glands of these guys when they were agitated was a deadly convulsant — lethal when injected on the tip of a blowgun dart. Not effective just rubbed on the skin, but I was never eager to take the chance of contamination through an abrasion or a small cut, so I pulled on the latex gloves....

And the red bulb on the radio-contact alert device flashed on.

Picos. He would wait ten minutes. I needed less than one. I stripped off the gloves. No skulking behind the cover of residence and storage shed this time. To hell with that pair of plotters. I was chief here. I strode up the middle of the compound. The oozy ground squished under my work boots. I slapped a film of mist droplets off my face. Wrenched open the radio room door and plunked my butt down at the transceiver. Flipped it on.

"Station Four. Come in, Picos."

Static. Then, "...Señor. Very bad flooding..." Static again. "You must..." Lost him.

Then I heard the door yanked open behind me, so hard it swung around to slam against the outside of the building.

"Very bad," Picos's gritty voice repeated. "Be ready to..."

I jerked my head around to glimpse two big hands rush at me. Yank me off the chair. I sprawled on the floorboards. Ted. He grabbed the transceiver, lifted it over his head, hurled it to the floor.

"This time it stays busted, Turkey!" He spun around, stepped to the door. I got my feet under me, shoved myself up, head pounding in fury.

"You dumb-ass son of a bitch..."

"Jesus, Turkey," he laughed from the doorway. "Such language!"

I threw myself at him. Crashed my shoulder into his good side, grappled him around the waist and rammed him out the door. All his weight plus mine jammed down on his bad hip. He let out a yell as we fell flat on the mucky sod outside.

I jumped to my feet and watched him struggle back up, groaning and gasping. Playing it big, I thought. The backs of his shirt and pants were black with oozing mud. His colossal ego had to be devastated. Mortally, I hoped.

"Get the hell away from here!" I shouted. "You and your crooked buddy. Take the damned canoe and get out of here! Today. NOW."

He stood on wobbly legs, feet shuffling for balance. His eyes bored into mine. Pure hatred.

"This time, you miserable bastard," I said icily, "you can honestly claim I pushed you. Get the hell out of my Station."

Eyes blazing, mouth compressed in a furious line, he swung away. I felt shaken. Then I felt damned good. I'd humbled the schoolyard bully. Knocked the domineering lard-brained favorite nephew of my boss flat on his sorry ass.

I put the battered transceiver back on its shelf. Plugged it back in. Tried turning it on. Not a glimmer. We were truly cut off. Mute—in the path of whatever Picos had so desperately tried to warn us about.

Resisting the temptation to strut, I hurried back to the lab. Passed the west end of the residence without a glance toward their room. But I wondered how Ted was explaining his mud-splattered slacks and shirt. All things considered, I was feeling pretty damned good about myself.

The morning had darkened to an almost twilight gloom, the low cloud cover a black quilt undulating close overhead. Thunder rolled like doom on hold. I hoped to God it would stay up there in the Acarai and Tumucumaque ranges.

But as I stepped back into the lab, rain lashed across the compound. I tried to remember what I'd been doing when the radio call light went on. Saw the latex gloves on the work table. The poison-dart frog aquarium. I pulled the gloves on again while I tried to collect myself. My brain raced in too many directions. Ted infuriated. McArt covetous. Agata confident about hiding her emerald. The gun. Where was the damned gun?

An immense flash left me seeing everything in negative. I shook my head as vision cleared. A thunderclap rattled the lab's framing, shivered the water in the eel's aquarium. A sudden rainburst battered the lab's metal roof.

The tumult in the mountains had begun to roll down the Trombetas.

24

At the lab's work shelf, I stared into the eerily gray, rain-swept compound. Squinted as lightning flared. The three 60-watt bulbs overhead flickered then steadied.

Calm down, Emmett. Concentrate on the best that can happen: Ted and McArt, spurred into action by the oncoming squall line, throw their gear together. Rush to the riverbank. Free the canoe from its tree lashings, heave it into the water on the dock's calmer down-current side. Not much of a challenge with the river's level—and the dock—now only a few feet below the bank's crest. And off they paddle, taking with them their bluster, bluff and bullshit. With luck, never to be seen or heard of again.

The only challenge Felicia, Agata, and I then faced would be weathering the oncoming storm. We would wade through a foot or so of flooding to reach the compound's higher ground and shelter in the storage building until the water receded back into the river. A reassuring scenario.

But as rain continued to rattle the lab roof, I couldn't shake a creepy feeling that something dreadful was about to shatter my hope for a civilized way out of all this. Maybe a little manual labor here in the lab could settle me down.

I pushed up from the shelf and stepped down the right-side walkway between the tanks along the north side frame-and-screen wall and the center-row tanks. Passed the Electrophorus eel, the puffers, stingrays, stone fish. Returned to the frogs' aquarium in the northwest corner. In their murky tank, the bright yellow Phyllobates were easy to spot. Pulled the latex gloves tight, reached in and took a frog in each hand. As if I'd closed a circuit, lightning flared hot white, so intense I could see nothing for a few seconds. I heard a bang behind me. For a panicky instant, I thought the lab had been struck. As thunder crashed uncomfortably close, I spun around.

Someone stood in the lab.

"It's time, Turkey."

Ted, rain-soaked, his voice almost comic in over-dramatic intensity. But there was nothing laughable about the pistol he held in his right hand, arm at his side, gun pointing downward, but no less frightening. With luck, I thought, not so inanely, the next lightning flash would startle this crazy bastard into shooting himself in the foot.

"So where did you hide that damned thing?" Maybe if I can get him talking, he would come to what few senses he might have left.

He gave me a lopsided smile. "In the latrine, Turkey. Down in a space between the two-by-fours behind the seat." He giggled. "The zapper was in the crapper."

"Why don't you just put the gun on the table, Ted? There's got to be a lot of water headed this way. You and McArt could still have enough time to get out of here in the canoe."

"You bet your sorry ass we're leaving in the canoe, but not until I…"

"Until what, Ted? Use the gun? You want to live with that the rest of your life?"

"You've already given me something to live with for the rest of my life. Now you're damned well going to pay for it."

"Ted, for God's sake, use your brain for once."

"I'm using it now." He stepped across the front of the lab to stand near the eel tank, awkwardly straddling the northside walkway. He raised the pistol and took a step toward me. Ice streaked up my spine, gripped my shoulders. My heart banged in my ears. There was nothing left of this guy but his stupid fixation on revenge for what he had done to himself.

"Ted, think!" I shouted "Listen to me! Go back to Philadelphia. Have a top surgeon take a look at that hip. You're a good-looking guy. Maybe acting really is your future. Try it again."

I was babbling, trying to divert him, jolt him away from his terrifying single purpose. But his wooden expression told me I was shouting at a mind-set wall.

He took another step toward me. And grinned. "I should have got St. John to say a prayer for you." Then he burst into laughter. "Jesus, Turkey, you're about to die and you're standing here in rubber gloves holding — what the hell are those?"

"Poison-dart frogs. That's why the gloves, Ted." And his disgusted grimace gave me a flicker of hope. "Remember? I told you their sweat can kill. And these little bastards are damned nervous."

"Say goodbye to your little froggies, Turkey." Just three paces away, he thrust the Colt straight at my heart.

"You say goodbye to them, Ted!" And I threw the frogs at his face.

He yelled and ducked away. One frog sailed past his right ear, bounced off the screen over the work shelf. The other hit Ted's left cheek. Just under his eye—and clung there.

He screamed. Both hands flew to his face. The pistol clattered to the walkway stones. Clawing at the persistent frog, he stumbled backward.

I dove for the gun, snatched it off the floor, jumped up and dropped it in the nearest aquarium—the electric eel's tank. Looked like a feat of superb planning, but it was my desperate reaction to panic.

I surely wasn't prepared for what happened next. Ted yanked the frog off his cheek and threw it across the lab. "You son of a bitch!" he shouted. He leaped to the Electrophorus tank and plunged his arm down for the gun on the aquarium's gravel. He didn't make it. His face froze. His eyes rolled back. A strangled scream gurgled in his throat as the eel's rapid fire electric shocks surged through him. His legs gave way. Arm still hooked deep in the tank, he pitched sideways and collapsed.

Under his weight, the big glass front panel cracked. In a roar of water and shattered glass, it shattered. Forty gallons cascaded over Ted's sprawled body. Riding the rush, the big eel flopped down on his chest. Six-hundred-volt pulses at hundreds of pulses per second surged through him. His eyes bulged. His legs and arms spasmed. His fingers twitched… barely twitched…stopped. He lay still.

I sagged against the puffer-fish tank, grabbed its rim for support. Overwhelmed by the enormity of what had just happened, I stared at the ghastly tableau. Ted's eyes stared at the roof. Not a blink. Not a hint of life.

What the hell should I do? Try artificial respiration? I stepped toward him, looked around wildly for something I might use to pry off the squirming eel…

Out in the compound, a scream. Ted's body blocked the narrow aisle. I whirled around, raced across the rear walkway and back up the far side. I was struck by the inane thought that wherever Ted was now, I was sure he blamed me for putting him there.

I threw open the door, stumbled, then dove into the storm's half light. Another scream. Felicia!

I sprinted toward the residence. She stood alone in the doorway, pointing toward the mess hut. I swung around. Lightning blazed again and spotlighted someone running through the compound's trees toward the residence. McArt. The thunderclap shook the Station. Another flash. A second rushing figure—Agata, close behind. In her hand something glittered. A knife.

"Gatuno!" she shrieked. "Bastardo!"

I rushed toward them. "He has mi emerald," she cried. "I will kill him!"

McArt's head swung my way. "Stay out of this!" he yelled. Smooth, duplicitous St. John had become brutal, thieving McArt.

"Ted!" he shouted. "Where the hell are you?"

"He's dead, McArt!"

"Dead?" He stopped short, stared at me. Big mistake. Agata rushed him from behind. "Mi emerald!" she screamed. And flew at him.

He whirled around and rammed his fist into her stomach. The knife glanced off his shoulder. With both hands, he grabbed for her throat and I slammed into him full tilt. He crashed down on his back.

The knife lay in the mud and I lunged for it.

His right leg flew up between mine, slammed into my crotch. I'd never felt such pain. My knees gave way. As I fell in agony, McArt scrabbled for the knife. Agata leaped on him from behind, snaked an arm around his neck, a bleeding arm, scored with shallow cuts. That bastard!

McArt reached back, grabbed her by the shoulders, crouched and flipped her over his head. She thudded down on her back. Gasped for breath.

McArt scrambled to his feet, the knife in his hand. He stood over Agata as she tried to sit up.

"You're dead, bitch!" he roared. Up went the blade.

"No!" Felicia screamed from the residence doorway. Now she was holding something.

McArt swung around, stared then laughed. "Oh, for God's sake, woman. Put that thing down."

"You put the knife down, you little shit." First time I'd ever heard her use that word. Her tone was chilling.

I struggled to my knees. Saw an enraged McArt turn back to grab Agata by the throat. He raised the knife again. I pushed myself up. Lunged for him. Heard a twang. He flung out his arm. The knife went sailing. He collapsed across Agata's legs.

What in hell? Then I saw the feathered shaft of Felicia's target arrow deep in McArt's back. I crouched over him, checked his wrist for a pulse. None. She must have hit him in the heart. For a long moment, no one said anything. I forced myself to yank McArt's body off Agata's legs. Helped her to her feet.

"He was a bad man, Senhor," she said in an amazingly calm voice. She reached down and pulled her pendant from McArt's shirt pocket. I looked at her injured arm. The bleeding had stopped, but the sadistic cuts must have...

"He made me tell where I hid it," Agata's tone was chilling. She touched her breast. In her bra, for Pete's sake? She picked up the knife, a serrated steak knife, apparently grabbed from a kitchen drawer by McArt, used to terrify her, then tossed aside as he reveled in possessing the emerald. A fatally overconfident trickster, he now lay dead at my feet. She stared at the knife. Picked it up. "He was a bad man, Senhor," she repeated quietly. "Muito bad."

Felicia ran toward us, her target bow still in her hand. "Oh, God, Emmett. How horrible! He was going to kill her. I had to. I had to."

I took her in my arms. "Yes, you did. You saved her...and probably saved me as well."

"I had to," she said again. "Had to..." She was shaken by sobs.

"Senhora." Agata grasped Felicia's hands in hers. "Senhora, senhora, Obrigado. I...thank you so much." She nodded disdainfully at McArt's body. "No tears for him, senhora. No tears."

Felicia shuddered. "He was such a conniving bastard."

"Not any more," I said.

She looked at me, horror in her face. "Emmett, I killed a man."

"You saved Agata's life, Felicia."

"But I...but I..."

I took her gently by the shoulders, looked straight into her tear-filled eyes. "Listen to me, Felicia. He was about to stab Agata to death. If you hadn't thought lightning fast and hadn't done what you did, she would be gone, and we would be facing this maniac with the knife in his hand. So thank God you thought fast. And weren't afraid to act."

"Emmett, I...what is that?"

The lightning and thunder had abated. But now I heard a chorus of distant shrieks.

"Senhora," Agata said, "those are porcos."

The wild shrieking grew louder. "Peccaries," I said. "Wild pigs. Stampeding. Coming this way." What would panic a herd of pigs, I wondered? Then I heard another sound—a rushing sound—not of wind. I heard the rumbling surge of oncoming water.

"Flash flood," I warned. "Coming downriver."

The wild pigs, dozens of them, burst across the far end of the compound; their hoofs vibrated the ground. Several tumbled in their haste to scramble south, away from the oncoming sound that panicked them. They were trampled beneath the pell-mell rush then jumped back to their feet to follow the others. Their squeals and snorts faded into the forest to the south.

Now the air vibrated with the increasing rush of water.

"Emmett!" Felicia's cry was shrill with near panic. "What should we do?"

"The ground's higher back at the storage shed. We're going up there. Now!"

"Look!" she cried. "The river!"

A swell of brown water surged around the north bend. But the gushing sound came not from the river. The tumbling rush came from the forest behind the lab. The surge had spread over the bank upstream and now rushed toward us. I heard trees and understory growth crashing down under its force.

A tangle of broken limbs and uprooted brush slammed into the compound, roiled toward the rear of the lab and mess hut...and us.

I fought to keep my feet as debris-laden water began to swirl around my knees. The onrush bumped McArt's body toward the residence building. Felicia broke toward the higher end of the compound.

"No, no!" Agata screamed, caught her arm and yanked her back. "Fer-de-lance!" She pointed at the five-foot gray-mottled snake squirming past only a couple of paces in front of Felicia. My skin crawled. Dozens of snakes writhed among the floating debris.

"We can't possibly wade through that," Felicia gasped.

Above the water's rush, I heard the crackle of breaking wood. With tons of water-churned debris ramming its north wall, the mess hut building — its kitchen and Agata's quarters — gave way. The structure slid off its foundation then crumpled. My frame-and-screen lab was next to go. The north side caved in. The roof plunged down on the aquarium rows. I was sickened by the sharp cracks of shattering glass tanks. Whatever survived of my deadly menagerie was being washed into the compound by the unstoppable flood. Tangled in the lab debris, Ted's body rolled toward us then disappeared under the rising water. The flood rammed McArt's corpse toward the residence then surged over him to slam into the residence building. It too collapsed.

I spun around to see the river's onrushing billow sweep over our riverbank, slam over the dock and smash our tree-lashed canoe into scrap wood. No escape by canoe. No way to reach the higher end of the compound without a very real chance of a painful, even fatal sting or bite. We were trapped here on the submerged riverbank.

As the current slowed, I watched the dock, shoved under by the surge, slowly reappear. A chunk of broken branch banged against my legs. I looked down. The water had reached my thighs. How much higher?

I stared at the river, trying to come up with some way — any way — out of this total disaster. The dock swung ponderously on its upstream line, its oil drum-flotation rigging bumped against the submerged crest of the bank.... Yes! Our only chance.

"The dock!" I yelled. "Get on the dock. Agata, we'll need that knife."

"Sim, Senhor."

I pointed at the taut upstream line. With quick understanding, she handed me the steak knife.

In the midst of all this mayhem and panic, my mind flashed to the research notes now, no doubt, soggy and unreadable in the lab's wreckage. The dozens of dangerous marine specimens set free among the crashing tanks and now swirling among us. All lost. No time to even think about that. We had to get out of here — and fast.

Alert for horrors underfoot, we pushed through the swirling water toward the dock. Not two yards away, I spotted a seven-foot snake

I couldn't identify. It undulated past, and we scrambled onto the dock's planking.

"Untie the slack line," I shouted to my two struggling women. "I'll cut the one up-current."

They easily unknotted the slack downriver line from its dock cleat. The other woven nylon line, held taut as wire to its nearly submerged upstream stake, began to give way to my frantic sawing.

As Felicia and Agata crawled to the dock's center, the line snapped away with a lurch that nearly catapulted all three of us into the river. The dock became a raft, buoyed on its tightly lashed empty oil drums. We whirled downstream, banged into a tree standing on the now-invisible riverbank. Fingers clawing the spaced planking, we held on desperately. The current pushed us past the south bend into less turbulent open water.

"We should make Oriximiná before dark," I told them. I stared at the knife still in my hand. It had drawn blood from Agata. It had come close to killing McArt then threatened Agata. Now it had saved us.

What had begun as an idyllic scientific assignment in the rain forest had ended in a nightmare.

I stabbed the knife into the planking.

***

"Emmett," Felicia said softly, "you couldn't have done anything about the flood."

"Not the flood. The rest of it. Ted, McArt." I hunched beside her, arm around her shoulders. Beneath her sopping blouse, I felt her tremble.

"Don't think about that," she said. "We're alive. That's all that counts."

There would be hell to pay up in Philadelphia. But she was right. And there was always Mote Marine — or that doctorate I should have tried for. I held her tighter, leaned back, bracing myself with my free arm. The air felt warmer; the sky was a lighter gray. The current smoothed into a steady rush southward. We had survived.

Behind me, I felt Agata's warm fingers close over my cold hand.

EPILOG

I was right. We reached Oriximiná before dark. But I was wrong thinking that was the end of our rafting trip. As we floated past, helpless in midstream, some good souls there sent word on to Óbidos thirty miles downstream. Just before night fell, a half-dozen daring power boaters threw us ropes. We hitched them to the dock cleats and were towed ashore, wet and worn out. An overly helpful rescuer contacted the Para Policia. Late the next morning, my old friend Capitão Rolha boated in from Santarém, took all three of us back there in his police boat—for our "convenience"—and his.

"Senhor Rebner was in the laboratory building when it collapsed," I told him. "Senhor McArt—the false 'doctor' from Tiago—was caught in the flood water that swept across the Station."

Truthful statements, both of them, but... My eyes on his, I waited for his reaction. He stroked the ends of his droopy mustache. I struggled not to blink. Then he shrugged. "You are free to go, Senhor Durkin. You, your wife and..."

I held my breath. Surely he hadn't forgotten his appearance at the Station in his search for the knife-wielding wife from Manaus.

"...And your criada—your servant. You are all three free to go."

He still accepted my lie about the date of Agata's arrival at the Station? Had he decided she was justified in defending herself against a brutal husband, despite his Manaus police affiliation? Or did Rolha decide our traumatic escape from certain disaster had been punishment enough for Agata—and for my merciful lie?

I thanked him and we rushed out of Santarém on the next flight to Belém. There Agata, tearful but determined, left us. She flew south. Felicia and I flew north, on one of Varig's three weekly flights to Miami.

Weeks later, the Foundation forwarded a letter from São Paulo. "I am sous chef at Hotel Gran Corona," Agata wrote. "I never forget what you did for me. Mi querido."

"What's 'querido'?" Felicia asked.

"'Good friend,' I think."

She gave me a long look. Then smiled, just a bit knowingly, I thought. "Friend," she said. Remarkable woman, my Felicia. Here in Sarasota, she is manager of Sandbar Arts, with a collection of her own rainforest sketches a featured attraction.

Before we returned to Sarasota and I to a fortunately open position at Mote Marine, the Foundation required my attendance as part of its investigation of the destruction of Station Four.

In the Foundation's boardroom, Oliver Rebner sat at the head of the huge, highly polished walnut table, chief "roo" in this not-for-profit style kangaroo court. The Foundation's eight directors flanked the table, four to a side. Among the director roos sat stolid and solid Bert Noonan, my father-in-law. I was seated at the table's foot, no doubt intended to feel like a joey. But I didn't feel like hopping away.

I was pissed.

Oliver tapped his pen on the table top. "The meeting will come to order. One agenda item only, today, gentlemen. The report of Station Four's former chief."

He glanced behind him, nodded. A middle-aged secretary, her graying hair in a severe bun, began scribbling minutes.

"Emmett, please summarize your submitted written report."

"Gladly." I cleared my throat. "The work at Station Four was compelling. I have not been apprised of its effectiveness or value to the Foundation."

Ho-hum expressions around the table.

"The facilities were rudimentary—especially for a scientific installation." Not so ho-hum now. "The flood water easily took them down, except for the storage building on its slightly higher ground. Had the demolished buildings been elevated only a few feet on pilings, they would still be standing today."

"Are you implying," asked a florid-faced director, "the Foundation stinted on the construction?"

"I'm not implying anything. I'm stating facts. Cheap design and construction doomed the Station."

"The flood doomed your Station, sir!" he snapped back.

"A glaring lack of consideration of annual rainy-season hazards contributed, sir."

"Emmett," Oliver put in hurriedly, "more to the point than a deliberation over construction specifications, I lost a nephew down there.

Your written report states he was crushed in the collapse of the laboratory. Was he working in there at the time?"

"After his first few days, he never worked in there."

"I sent him to work there, Emmett."

"Do you or do you not want the details?" I struggled to keep my voice level.

Oliver hesitated. "I thought I had the details of his work there from Ted."

"Did he include the incident on the riverbank?"

Oliver glanced around the table. All eyes were on him now, and I knew the board members had no idea what we were talking about.

A director with a neatly trimmed mustache and goatee lifted a hand.

"Dr. Larue?"

"I understand, Oliver, your nephew, Theodore, had a fall that incapacitated him."

He turned to me. "Was that why he didn't work in the lab with you?"

"If you want the truth, gentlemen—and I assume you do—Ted was far more interested in my wife than in the lab specimens."

In the silence, Felicia's father gaped at me.

Oliver swung around to the secretary. "You will strike that, Ms. Spencer. And take no more minutes until I say otherwise." He turned back to me. "Now, Emmett, you're making quite an accusation. Might you care to rephrase what you just said?"

"What I said is what happened. Your nephew had no interest whatever in working at Station Four. He was screwing around on the riverbank. When I tried to save him from falling during a silly show-off jig of his, he accused me of pushing him down the bank. He returned from the hospital in Belém with a Colt pistol he had bought in a street market there. He told me he bought it to kill me."

"My God!" one of the directors muttered.

"Stop right there, Emmett," Oliver ordered. "My nephew is dead. The result of an unfortunate accident. I see no value in your continuing these sordid allegations." He looked around the table. "Any questions, gentlemen?"

"I have a question, Mr. Chairman."

Oliver glared at me. "You have a question?"

"Just one." I had the full board's attention. "Give me just one specific example of how any of the dozens of specimens I sent you have been used."

Oliver looked at me, expressionless. "Classified."

"Classified? Withheld from the guy who sweated blood down there in jungle hell to get it to you?"

In the dead silence, Oliver cleared his throat. "You were paid, Durkin. Well paid."

"Paid to keep quiet?"

"What the hell does that mean?" goateed Dr. Larue demanded.

With outstretched palms-down hands, Oliver made dampening motions. "Gentlemen, gentlemen."

"Don't 'gentlemen' me, Oliver," Dr. Larue said. "You know damned well any adverse publicity…"

"What's 'adverse' about what the Foundation does?" I asked.

"Jesus, Emmett," my father-in-law burst out. "We live on publicity. Positive publicity."

"Bert!" Oliver's tone was lethal. "Shut up!"

Everyone at the table stared at him.

"I mean…what I mean… My apologies, Bert. I got a bit carried away. I'm sure you know my concern. Our concern."

"My concern," I told them, "is I think I know what's going on here."

"If you're thinking of going public with it," Oliver said, his tone now remarkably genial, "think again. Apparently you didn't read the fine print in your contract. Clause 19: 'Party of the second part—' that's you— 'hereby agrees not to disclose information concerning the Foundation or its activities during the term of his/her employment or thereafter, under penalty of forfeiture of all monies paid to him/her to the date of such unauthorized disclosure.' Enough said, Durkin?"

"Not quite." I reached into my jacket pocket, pulled out an envelope and tossed it on the table. "My resignation. I'd rather work for peanuts at a respectable research organization than one that uses 'research' as a fund-raising front."

I nodded at the stunned faces around the table. "Gentlemen," I said with a little smile. And I walked out.

***

I left Foundation headquarters with a feeling of relief, but I knew the fallout of the disaster at Station Four was not yet ended. The Para Policia were sure to investigate the site. After the rains subsided, the battered remnants must be exposed — and the two bodies.

Felicia and I flew to Sarasota in a state of suspense. Two weeks later, I received a Philadelphia-postmarked envelope with no return address. Possibly from one of the less bitterly disposed Foundation directors? In it: a clipping from the *Philadelphia Inquirer*. According to the Associated Press, an inspection of the Rebner Foundation's Brazil-based Research Station Four revealed a badly decomposed body, identified through Internet-supplied dental records as that of Theodore Rebner, nephew of the Philadelphia-based Rebner Foundation. Cause of death: drowning.

One body? No second corpse with an arrow in its back? Had the remains of St. John-McCure-McArt been carried off by a helpful jaguar? Perhaps borne deep into the understory by the wreckage-choked surge across the compound?

Case closed, thank God. Except...except for one more uncertainty. Had the Station's mission truly been one of research potentially valuable to medical interests? To the military? Or, as I suspected, were Station Four and the other three such installations no more than bare-bones charades to keep grants and donations flowing?

Felicia and I might never know. Yet down in the wilderness along the treacherous Trombetas, we did make a discovery of lasting value.

Amidst the strains, stresses and flagrant behaviors of that tropical sojourn, we discovered we truly loved each other.

END

If you enjoyed Bill Hallstead's book *River of Madness,* may we suggest you try his other titles published by BluewaterPress LLC?

Germany's use of the great Zeppelins in World War I marked the very first time aerial strategic bombing took place in the world. It was a terrible way to wage war. For the British, it was horrible on the ground underneath the behemoths dropping their bombs.

For the Germans flying the great airships, survival became a daily question. Using this historical time as a backdrop, William Hallstead penned a novel of action, adventure, intrigue, love, and espionage.

Another fantastic novel from the mind of storyteller Bill Hallstead is his tale of Rod Montgomery in *Hard Days in Paradise*.

Elrod "Rod" Montgomery (please don't call him Elrod), a Philadelphia private investigator, had thought a visit from the IRS to inspect his home office would be his only major headache that fateful day, until he received a call from a Florida Public Defender.

Apparently, his ex-partner, Stanley McKance, who disappeared with all $20,000 of the partnership's money two years previously, was alive and well in a South Florida jail — charged with murder. Irene Hutchins, Esq. was calling to enlist the aid of Stan's old "buddy" in proving that he didn't do it.

www.ingramcontent.com/pod-product-compliance
Lightning Source LLC
Chambersburg PA
CBHW030509260626
47157CB00005B/1717